Phoebe Cary

Poems of Faith, Hope, and Love

Phoebe Cary

Poems of Faith, Hope, and Love

ISBN/EAN: 9783337090067

Printed in Europe, USA, Canada, Australia, Japan

Cover: Foto ©Andreas Hilbeck / pixelio.de

More available books at **www.hansebooks.com**

POEMS

OF

ITH, HOPE, AND LOVE.

BY

PHŒBE CARY.

NEW YORK:
PUBLISHED BY HURD AND HO
459 BROOME STREET.
1868.

CONTENTS.

CONTENTS.

A MONKISH LEGEND.

EAUTIFUL stories, by tongue and
     pen.
     Are told of holy women and men,
     Who have heard, entranced in
        some lonely cell,
The things not lawful for lip to tell;
And seen. when their souls were caught away,
     What they might not say.

But one of the sweetest in tale or rhyme
Is told of a monk of the olden time,
Who read all day in his sacred nook
The words of the good Saint Austin's book,
Where he tells of the city of God, that best
     Last place of rest.

Sighing. the holy father said.
As he shut the volume he had read:
"Methinks if heaven shall only be
A Sabbath long as eternity.
Its bliss will at last be a weary reign,
     And its peace be pain."

1

So he wandered, musing under his hood,
Far into the depths of a solemn wood;
Where a bird was singing, so soft and clear,
That he paused and listened with charmèd
     ear;
Listened, nor knew, while thus intent.
     How the moments went.

But the music ceased, and the sweet spell broke,
And as if from a guilty dream he woke,
That holy man, and he cried aghast,
" *Mea culpa!* an hour has passed,
And I have not counted my beads, nor prayed
     To the saints for aid!"

Then, amazed he fled; but his horror grew,
For the wood was strange, and the pathway
     new;
Yet, with trembling step, he hurried on,
Till at last the open plain was won,
Where, grim and black, o'er the vale around,
     The convent frowned.

" Holy Saint Austin!" cried the monk,
And down on the ground for terror sunk;
For lo! the convent, tower, and cell,
Sacred crucifix, blessèd bell,
Had passed away, and in their stead,
     Was a ruin spread.

In that hour, while the rapture held him fast,
A century had come and passed;
And he rose an altered man, and went
His way, and knew what the vision meant;
For a mighty truth, till then unknown,
  By that trance was shown.

And he saw how the saints, with their Lord,
  shall say,
A thousand years are but as a day;
Since bliss itself must grow from bliss,
And holiness from holiness;
And love, while eternity's ages move,
  Cannot tire of love!

A WEARY HEART.

Ye winds, that talk among the pines,
   In pity whisper soft and low;
And from my trailing garden vines,
   Bear the faint odors as ye go;

Take fragrance from the orchard trees,
   From the meek violet in the dell;
Gather the honey that the bees
   Have left you in the lily's bell;

Pass tenderly as lovers pass,
   Stoop to the clover-blooms your wings,
Find out the daisies in the grass,
   The sweets of all insensate things;

With muffled feet, o'er beds of flowers,
   Go through the valley to the height,
Where frowning walls and lofty towers
   Shut in a weary heart to-night;

Go comfort her, who fain would give
   Her wealth below, her hopes above,
For the wild freedom that ye have
   To kiss the humblest flower ye love!

A GOOD DAY.

EARTH seems as peaceful and as bright
    As if the year that might not stay,
Had made a sweet pause in her flight,
    To keep another Sabbath day.

And I, as past the moments roll,
    Forgetting human fear and doubt,
Hold better Sabbath, in my soul,
    Than that which Nature holds without.

Help me, O Lord, if I shall see
    Times when I walk from hope apart,
Till all my days but seem to be
    The troubled week-days of the heart.

Help me to find, in seasons past,
    The hours that have been good or fair,
And bid remembrance hold them fast,
    To keep me wholly from despair.

Help me to look behind, before,
    To make my past and future form
A bow of promise, meeting o'er
    The darkness of my day of storm.

THE HERO OF FORT WAGNER.

Fort Wagner! that is a place for us
To remember well. my lad!
For us, who were under the guns, and know
The bloody work we had.

I should not speak to one so young,
Perhaps, as I do to you;
But you are a soldier's son, my boy,
And you know what soldiers do.

And when peace comes to our land again,
And your father sits in his home,
You will hear such tales of war as this,
For many a year to come.

We were repulsed from the Fort, you know,
And saw our heroes fall,
Till the dead were piled in bloody heaps
Under the frowning wall.

Yet crushed as we were and beaten back,
Our spirits never bowed;
And gallant deeds that day were done
To make a soldier proud.

Brave men were there, for their country's sake
  To spend their latest breath;
But the bravest was one who gave his life
  And his body after death.

No greater words than his dying ones
  Have been spoken under the sun;
Not even his, who brought the news
  On the field at Ratisbon.

I was pressing up, to try if yet
  Our men might take the place,
And my feet had slipped in his oozing blood
  Before I saw his face.

His face! it was black as the skies o'erhead
  With the smoke of the angry guns;
And a gash in his bosom showed the work
  Of our country's traitor sons.

Your pardon, my poor boy! I said,
  I did not see you here;
But I will not hurt you as I pass;
  I 'll have a care; no fear!

He smiled; he had only strength to say
  These words, and that was all:
" I 'm done gone, Massa; step on me;
  And you can scale the wall!"

COMING HOME.

O BROTHERS and sisters, growing old,
   Do you all remember yet
That home, in the shade of the rustling trees,
   Where once our household met?

Do you know how we used to come from school,
   Through the summer's pleasant heat;
With the yellow fennel's golden dust
   On our tired little feet?

And how sometimes in an idle mood
   We loitered by the way;
And stopped in the woods to gather flowers,
   And in the fields to play;

Till warned by the deep'ning shadow's fall,
   That told of the coming night,
We climbed to the top of the last, long hill,
   And saw our home in sight!

And, brothers and sisters, older now
   Than she whose life is o'er,
Do you think of the mother's loving face,
   That looked from the open door?

Alas, for the changing things of time;
  That home in the dust is low ;
And that loving smile was hid from us,
  In the darkness, long ago !

And we have come to life's last hill,
  From which our weary eyes
Can almost look on the home that shines
  Eternal in the skies.

So, brothers and sisters, as we go,
  Still let us move as one,
Always together keeping step,
  Till the march of life is done.

For that mother, who waited for us here,
  Wearing a smile so sweet,
Now waits on the hills of paradise
  For her children's coming feet !

MANY MANSIONS.

Her silver lamp half-filled with oil,
Night came, to still the day's turmoil,
And bring a respite from its toil.

Gliding about with noiseless tread,
Her white sheets on the ground she spread,
That wearied men might go to bed.

No watch was there for me to keep,
Yet could I neither rest nor sleep,
A recent loss had struck so deep.

I felt as if Omnipotence
Had given us no full recompense
For all the ills of time and sense.

So I went, wandering silently,
Where a great river sought the sea;
And fashioned out the life to be.

It was not drawn from book or creed,
And yet, in very truth and deed,
It answered to my greatest need.

And satisfied myself, I thought,
A heaven so good and perfect ought
To give to each what all have sought.

Near where I slowly chanced to stray,
A youth, and old man, worn and gray,
Down through the silence took their way;

And the night brought within my reach,
As each made answer unto each,
Some portion of their earnest speech.

The patriarch said: "Of all we know,
Or all that we can dream below,
Of that far land to which we go,

"This one assurance hath expressed,
To me, its blessedness the best —
'He giveth his beloved rest.'"

And the youth answered: "If it be
A place of inactivity,
It cannot be a heaven to me.

"Surely its joy must be to lack
These hindrances that keep us back
From rising on a shining track;

" Where each shall find his own true height,
Though in our place, and in our light,
We differ as the stars of night."

I listened, till they ceased to speak ;
And my heart answered, faint and weak,
Their heaven is not the heaven I seek !

Yet their discourse awoke again
Some hidden memories that had lain
Long undisturbed within my brain.

For oft, when bowed earth's care beneath,
I had asked others of their faith
In the life following after death ;

And what that better world could be,
Where, from mortality set free,
We put on immortality.

And each in his reply had shown
That he had shaped and made his own
By the best things which he had known ;

Or fashioned it to heal the woe
Of some great sorrow, which below
It was his hapless lot to know.

A mother once had said to me,
Over her dead: "My heaven will be
An undivided family."

One sick with mortal doubts and fears,
With looking blindly through her tears,
The way that she had looked for years,

Told me: "That world could have no pain,
Since there we should not wait in vain
For feet that will not come again."

A lover dreamed that heaven would be
Life's hour of perfect ecstacy,
Drawn out into eternity!

Men bending to their hopeless doom,
Toiling as in a living tomb,
Down shafts of everlasting gloom,

Out of the dark had answered me:
"Where there is light for us to see
Each other's faces, heaven must be."

An aged man, who bowed his head
With reverence o'er the page, and read
The words that ancient prophets said,

Talked of a glory never dim,
Of the veiled face of cherubim,
And harp, and everlasting hymn;

Saw golden streets and glittering towers —
Saw peaceful valleys, white with flowers,
Kept never-ending Sabbath hours.

One, who the cruel sea had crossed,
And seen, through billows madly tossed,
Great shipwrecks, where brave souls were lost,

Thus of the final voyage spake :
" Coming to heaven must be to make
Safe port, and no more journeys take."

And now their words of various kind
Come back to my bewildered mind,
And my faith staggered, faint and blind,

One moment ; then this truth seemed plain,
These have not trusted God in vain ;
To ask of Him must be to gain.

Every imaginable good,
We, erring. sinful, mortal, would
Give our belovèd, if we could ;

And shall not He, whose care enfolds
Our life, and all our way controls,
Yet satisfy our longing souls?

Since mortal step hath never been,
And mortal eye hath never seen,
Past death's impenetrable screen,

Who shall dare limit Him above,
Or tell the ways in which He 'll prove
Unto His children all His love ?

Then joy through all my being spread,
And, comforted myself, I said:
Oh, weary world, be comforted !

Souls, in your quest of bliss grown weak —
Souls, whose great woe no words can speak —
Not always shall ye vainly seek !

Men whose whole lives have been a night,
Shall come from darkness to the light;
Wanderers shall hail the land in sight.

Old saints, and martyrs of the Lamb,
Shall rise to sing their triumph psalm,
And wear the crown, and bear the palm.

And the pale mourner, with bowed head,
Who, for the living lost, or dead,
Here weeps, shall there be gently led,

To feel, in that celestial place,
The tears wiped softly from her face,
And know love's comforting embrace.

So shall we all, who groan in this,
Find, in that new life's perfectness,
Our own peculiar heaven of bliss —

More glorious than our faith believed,
Brighter than dreams our hope has weaved,
Better than all our hearts conceived.

Therefore will I wait patiently,
Trusting, where all God's mansions be,
There hath been one prepared for me;

And go down calmly to death's tide,
Knowing, when on the other side
I wake, I shall be satisfied.

HIDDEN SORROW.

HE has gone at last; yet I could not see
    When he passed to his final rest;
For he dropped asleep as quietly
    As the moon drops out of the west.

And I only saw, though I kept my place,
    That his mortal life was o'er,
By the look of peace across his face,
    That never was there before.

Sorrow he surely had in the past,
    Yet he uttered never a breath;
His lips were sealed in life as fast
    As you see them sealed in death.

Why he went from the world I do not know,
    Hiding a grief so deep;
But I think, if he ever had told his woe,
    He had found a better sleep.

For our trouble must some time see the light,
    And our anguish will have way;
And the infant, crying out in the night,
    Reveals what it hid by day.

2

And just like a needful, sweet relief
  To that bursting heart it seems,
When the little child's unspoken grief
  Runs into its pretty dreams.

And I think, though his face looks hushed and
    mild,
  And his slumber seems so deep,
He will sob in his grave, as a little child
  Keeps sobbing on in its sleep.

A WOMAN'S CONCLUSIONS.

I SAID, if I might go back again
  To the very hour and place of my birth;
Might have my life whatever I chose,
  And live it in any part of the earth;

Put perfect sunshine into my sky,
  Banish the shadow of sorrow and doubt;
Have all my happiness multiplied,
  And all my suffering stricken out;

If I could have known in the years now gone,
  The best that a woman comes to know;
Could have had whatever will make her blest,
  Or whatever she thinks will make her so;

Have found the highest and purest bliss
  That the bridal-wreath and ring inclose;
And gained the one out of all the world,
  That my heart as well as my reason chose:

And if this had been, and I stood to-night
  By my children, lying asleep in their beds
And could count in my prayers, for a rosary,
  The shining row of their golden heads;

Yea! I said, if a miracle such as this
    Could be wrought for me, at my bidding, still
I would choose to have my past as it is,
    And to let my future come as it will!

I would not make the path I have trod
    More pleasant or even, more straight or wide;
Nor change my course the breadth of a hair,
    This way or that way, to either side.

My past is mine, and I take it all;
    Its weakness — its folly, if you please;
Nay, even my sins, if you come to that,
    May have been my helps, not hindrances!

If I saved my body from the flames
    Because that once I had burned my hand;
Or kept myself from a greater sin
    By doing a less — you will understand;

It was better I suffered a little pain,
    Better I sinned for a little time,
If the smarting warned me back from death,
    And the sting of sin withheld from crime.

Who knows its strength, by trial, will know
    What strength must be set against a sin;
And how temptation is overcome
    He has learned, who has felt its power within!

And who knows how a life at the last may show?
   Why, look at the moon from where we stand!
Opaque, uneven, you say; yet it shines,
   A luminous sphere, complete and grand!

So let my past stand, just as it stands,
   And let me now, as I may, grow old;
I am what I am, and my life for me
   Is the best — or it had not been, I hold.?

ANSWERED.

I THOUGHT to find some healing clime
    For her I loved; she found that shore,
That city, whose inhabitants
    Are sick and sorrowful no more.

I asked for human love for her;
    The Loving knew how best to still
The infinite yearning of a heart,
    Which but infinity could fill.

Such sweet communion had been ours
    I prayed that it might never end;
My prayer is more than answered; now
    I have an angel for my friend.

I wished for perfect peace, to soothe
    The troubled anguish of her breast;
And, numbered with the loved and called,
    She entered on untroubled rest.

Life was so fair a thing to her,
    I wept and pleaded for its stay:
My wish was granted me, for lo!
    She hath eternal life to-day.

DISENCHANTED.

THE time has come, as I knew it must,
  She said, when we should part,
But I ceased to love when I ceased to trust,
  And you cannot break my heart.

Nay, I know not even if I am sad,
  And it must be for the best,
Since you only take what I thought I had,
  And leave to me the rest.

Not all the stars of my hope are set,
  Though one is in eclipse;
And I know there is truth in the wide world yet,
  If it be not on your lips.

And though I have loved you, who can tell
  If you ever had been so dear,
But that my heart was prodigal
  Of its wealth, and you were near.

I brought each rich and beautiful thing
  From my love's great treasury;
And I thought in myself to make a king
  With the robes of royalty.

But you lightly laid my honors down,
   And you taught me thus to know,
Not every head can wear the crown,
   That the hands of love bestow.

So, take whatever you can from me,
   And leave me as you will;
The dear romance and the poesy
   Were mine, and I have them still.

I have them still; and even now,
   When my fancy has her way,
She can make a king of such as thou,
   Or a god of common clay.

WINTER FLOWERS.

THOUGH Nature's lonesome, leafless bowers,
  With Winter's awful snows are white,
The tender smell of leaves and flowers
  Makes May-time in my room to-night:

While some, in homeless poverty,
  Shrink moaning from the bitter blast;
What am I, that my lines should be
  In good and pleasant places cast?

When other souls despairing stand,
  And plead with famished lips to-day,
Why is it that a loving hand
  Should scatter blossoms in my way?

O flowers, with soft and dewy eyes,
  To God my gratitude reveal;
Send up your incense to the skies
  And utter, for me, what I feel!

O innocent roses, in your buds
  Hiding for very modesty;
O violets, smelling of the woods,
  Thank Him, with all your sweets for me!

And tell Him, I would give this hour
All that is mine of good beside,
To have the pure heart of a flower,
That has no stain of sin to hide.

ARTHUR'S WIFE.

I 'm getting better, Miriam, though it tires me
      yet to speak ;
And the fever, clinging to me, keeps me spirit-
      less and weak,
And leaves me with a headache always when
      it passes off;
But I'm better, almost well at last, except this
      wretched cough !

I should have passed the livelong day alone
      here but for you ;
For Arthur never comes till night, he has so
      much to do!
And so sometimes I lie and think, till my heart
      seems nigh to burst,
Of the hope that lit my future, when I watched
      his coming first.

I wonder why it is that now he does not seem
      the same ;
Perhaps my fancy is at fault, and he is not to
      blame ;
It surely cannot be because he has me always
      near,

For I feared and felt it long before the time
  he brought me here.

Yet still, I said, his wife will charm each
  shadow from his brow,
What can I do to win his love, or prove my loving now ?
So I waited, studying patiently his every look
  and thought ;
But I fear that I shall never learn to please him
  as I ought.

I've tried so many ways to smooth his path
  where it was rough,
But I always either do too much, or fail to do
  enough ;
And at times, as if it wearied him, he pushes
  off my arm —
The very things that used to please have somehow lost their charm.

Once, when I wore a pretty gown, a gown he
  use to praise,
I asked him, laughing, if I seemed the sweetheart of old days.
He did not know the dress, and said, he never
  could have told,
'T was not that unbecoming one, which made me
  look so old !

I cannot tell how any thing I do may seem
    to him.
Sometimes he thinks me childish, and sometimes
    stiff and prim ;
Yet you must not think I blame him, dear ; I
    could not wrong him so —
He is very good to me, and I am happy, too,
    you know !

But I am often troublesome, and sick too much,
    I fear,
And sometimes let the children cry when he is
    home to hear.
Ah me ! if I should leave them, with no other
    care than his !
Yet he says his love is wiser than my foolish
    fondness is.

I think he 'd care about the babe. I called him
    Arthur, too —
Hoping to please him when I said, I named
    him, love, for you !
He never noticed any child of mine, except this
    one,
So the girls would only have to do as they have
    always done.

Give me my wrapper, Miriam. Help me a little,
    dear !

When Arthur comes home, vexed and tired, he
    must not find me here.
Why, I can even go down-stairs : I always make
    the tea.
He does not like that any one should wait on
    him but me.

He never sees me lying down when he is home,
    you know,
And I seldom tell him how I feel, he hates to
    hear it so ;
Yet I'm sure he grieves in secret at the thought
    that I may die,
Though he often laughs at me. and says,
    " You're stronger now than I."

Perhaps there are some men who love more
    than they ever say :
He does not show his feelings, but that may
    not be his way.
Why, how foolishly I'm talking, when I know
    he's good and kind !
But we women always ask too much ; more
    than we ever find.

My slippers, Miriam ! No, not those ; bring me
    the easy pair.
I surely heard the door below ; I hear him on
    the stair !

There comes the old, sharp pain again, that
    almost makes me frown ;
And it seems to me I always cough when I try
    to keep it down.   .

Ah, Arthur! take this chair of mine ; I feel so
    well and strong ;
Besides. I am getting tired of it — I've sat here
    all day long.
Poor dear! you work so hard for me, and I'm
    so useless. too !
A trouble to myself, and, worse, a trouble now
    to you.

ALAS!

Since, if you stood by my side to-day,
    Only our hands could meet,
What matter that half the weary world
    Lies out between our feet;

That I am here by the lonesome sea.
    You by the pleasant Rhine? —
Our hearts were just as far apart
    If I held your hand in mine!

Therefore. with never a backward glance,
    I leave the past behind;
And standing here by the sea alone,
    I give it to the wind.

I give it all to the cruel wind,
    And I have no word to say;
Yet, alas! to be as we have been,
    And to be as we are to-day!

MOTHER AND SON.

BRIGHTLY for him the future smiled,
  The world was all untried;
He had been a boy, almost a child,
  In your household till he died.

And you saw him, young and strong and fair,
  But yesterday depart;
And now you know he is lying there
  Shot to death through the heart!

Alas, for the step so proud and true
  That struck on the war-path's track;
Alas, to go, as he went from you,
  And to come, as they brought him back!

One shining curl from that bright young head,
  Held sacred in your home,
Is all you will have to keep in his stead
  In the years that are to come.

You may claim of his beauty and his youth
  Only this little part —
It is not much with which to staunch
  The wound in a mother's heart!

3

It is not much with which to dry
    The bitter tears that flow;
Not much in your empty hands to lie
    As the seasons come and go.

Yet he has not lived and died in vain,
    For proudly you may say,
He has left a name, with never a stain
    For your tears to wash away.

And evermore shall your life be blest,
    Though your treasures now are few,
Since you gave for your country's good the best
    God ever gave to you!

COMPLAINT.

"Though we were parted, or though he had
    died,"
She said, "I could bear the worst,
If he only had loved me at the last,
    As he loved me at the first.

"But woe is me!" said the hapless maid,
    "That ever a lover came;
Since he who lit in my heart the fire,
    Has failed to tend the flame.

"Ah! why did he pour in my life's poor cup
    A nectar so divine,
If he had no power to fill it up
    With a draught as pure and fine?

"Why did he give me one holiday,
    Then send me back to toil?
Why did he set a lamp in my house,
    And leave it lacking oil?

"Why did he plant the rose in my cheeks
    When he knew it could not thrive —

That the dew of kisses, only, keeps
The true blush-rose alive?

" If he tired so soon of the song I sung
In our love's delicious June,
Why did he set the thoughts of my heart
All to one blessèd tune?

" Oh, if he were either true or false,
My torment might have end:
He hath been, for a lover, too unkind;
Too loving for a friend!

" And there is not a soul in all the world
So wretched as mine must be,
For I cannot live on his love," she said,
" Nor die of his cruelty."

TRUE LOVE.

I THINK true love is never blind,
  But rather brings an added light;
An inner vision quick to find
  The beauties hid from common sight.

No soul can ever clearly see   .
  Another's highest, noblest part;
Save through the sweet philosophy
  And loving wisdom of the heart.

Your unanointed eyes shall fall
  On him who fills my world with light;
You do not see my friend at all,
  You see what hides him from your sight.

I see the feet that fain would climb,
  You, but the steps that turn astray :
I see the soul unharmed, sublime;
  You, but the garment, and the clay.

You see a mortal, weak, misled,
  Dwarfed ever by the earthly clod;
I see how manhood, perfected,
  May reach the stature of a god.

Blinded I stood, as now you stand,
   Till on mine eyes, with touches sweet,
Love, the deliverer, laid his hand,
   And lo ! I worship at his feet !

THEODORA.

By that name you will not know her,
But if words of mine can show her
In such way that you may see
How she doth appear to me;
If, attending you shall find
The fair picture in my mind,
You will think this title meetest,
Gift of God, the best and sweetest.

All her free, impulsive acting,
Is so charming, so distracting,
Lovers think her made, I know,
Only for a play-fellow.
Coral lips, concealing pearls
Hath she, 'twixt dark rows of curls ;
And her words, dropt soft and slowly,
Seem half ravishing, half holy.

She is for a saint too human,
Yet too saintly for a woman ;
Something childish in her face
Blended with maturer grace,
Shows a nature pure and good,
Perfected by motherhood ; —

Eyes Madonna-like, love-laden,
Holier than befit a maiden.

Simple in her faith unshrinking,
Wise as sages in her thinking;
Showing in her artless speech
All she of herself can teach;
Hiding love and thought profound,
In such depths as none may sound;
One, though known and comprehended,
Yet with wondrous mystery blended.

Sitting meekly and serenely,
Sitting in a state most queenly;
Knowing, though dethroned, discrowned,
That her kingdom shall be found;
That her Father's child must be
Heir of immortality;
This is still her highest merit,
That she ruleth her own spirit.

Thou to whom is given this treasure,
Guard it, love it without measure;
If forgotten it should lie
In a weak hand carelessly,
Thou mayst wake to miss and weep,
That which thou didst fail to keep;
Crying, when the gift is taken,
" I am desolate, forsaken ! "

UP AND DOWN.

The sun of a sweet summer morning
  Smiled joyously down from the sky,
As we climbed up the mountain together, —
  My charming companion and I ;
The wild birds that live in the bushes
  Sang love, without fear or disguise,
And the flowers, with soft, blushing faces,
  Looked love from their wide-open eyes.

In and out, through the sunshine and shadow,
  We went where the odors are sweet ;
And the pathway that led from the valley
  Was pleasant and soft to our feet :
And while we were hopefully talking —
  For our hearts and our thoughts seemed
        in tune —
Unaware, we had climbed to the summit,
  And the sun of the morning, to noon.

For my genial and pleasant companion
  Was so kind and so helpful the while,
That I felt how the path of a lifetime
  Might be brightened and cheered by his
        smile ;

And how blest, with his care and his guid-
    ance,
  Some true, loving woman might be, —
Of course, never hoping or wishing
  Such fortune would happen to me!

We spoke of life, death, truth, and friend-
    ship, —
  Things hoped for, below and above,
And then, sitting down at the summit,
  We talked about loving, and love;
And he told me the years of his lifetime
  Till now had been barren and drear,
In tones that were touching and tender
  As exquisite music to hear.

And I saw in the eyes looking on me,
  A meaning that could not be hid,
Till I blushed — Oh, it makes me so angry,
  Even now, to remember I did! —
As, taking my hand, he drew nearer,
  And said, in his tenderest tone,
'T was like the dear hand that so often
  Had lovingly lain in his own.

And that, 't was not flattery only,
  But honest and merited praise,
To say I resembled his sweetheart
  Sometimes in my words and my ways;

That I had the same womanly feelings,
　My thoughts were as noble and high ;
But that she was a trifle, say, fairer,
　And a year or two younger than I.

Then he told me my welfare was dearer
　To him than I might understand,
And he wished he knew any one worthy
　To claim such a prize as my hand ;
And his darling, I surely must love her,
　Because she was charming and good,
And because she had made him so happy ;
　And I said I was sure that I should —

That nothing could make me so happy
　As seeing him happy ; but then
I was wretchedly tired and stupid,
　And wished myself back in the glen.
That the sun, so delightful at morning,
　Burned now with a merciless flame ;
And I dreaded again to go over
　The long, weary way that we came.

So we started to go down the mountain ;
　But the wild birds, the poor silly things,
Had finished their season of courting,
　And put their heads under their wings ;
And the flowers that opened at morning,
　All blushing with joy and surprise,

Had turned from the sun's burning glances,
　And sleepily shut up their eyes.

Every thing I had thought so delightful
　Was gone, leaving scarcely a trace;
And even my charming companion
　Grew stupid and quite commonplace.
He was not the same man that I thought him —
　I can't divine why; but at once,
The fellow, who had been so charming
　Was changed from a dear to a dunce.

But if any young man needs advising,
　Let me whisper a word in his ear : —
Don't talk of the lady that 's absent
　Too much to the lady that 's near.
My kindness is disinterested;
　So in speaking to me never mind;
But the course I advise you to follow
　Is safe, as a rule, you will find.

You may talk about love in the abstract,
　Say the ladies are charming and dear;
But you need not select an example,
　Nor say she is there, or is here.
When it comes to that last application,
　Just leave it entirely out,
And give to the lady that 's present
　The benefit still of the doubt!

BEYOND.

When you would have sweet flowers to smell
    and hold,
You do not seek them underneath the cold
Close-knitted sod, that hides away the mould;
   Where in the spring-time past
   The precious seed was cast.

Not down, but up, you turn your eager eyes;
You find in summer the fair flowery prize
On the green stalk, that reaches towards the
    skies,
   And, bending down its top,
   Gather the fragrant crop.

If you would find the goal of some pure rill,
That, following her unrestrainèd will,
Runs laughing down the bright slope of the hill,
   Or, with a serious mien,
   Walks through the valley green,

You do not seek the spot where she was born,
The cavernous mountain chamber, dim, forlorn,
That never saw the fair face of the morn,
   Where she, with wailing sound,
   First started from the ground;

But rather will you track her windings free,
To where at last she rushes eagerly
Into the white arms of her love, the sea,
   And hides in his embrace
   The rapture on her face!

If, from the branches of a neigboring tree,
A bird some morn were missing suddenly,
That all the summer sang for ecstasy,
   And made your season seem
   Like a melodious dream,

You would not search about the leafless dell,
In places where the nestling used to dwell,
To find the white walls of her broken shell,
   Thinking your child of air,
   Your wingèd joy, was there!

But rather, hurrying from the autumn gale,
Your feet would follow summer's flowery trail
To find her spicy grove, and odorous vale;
   Knowing that birds and song
   To pleasant climes belong.

Then wherefore, when you see a soul set free
From this poor seed of its mortality,
And know you sow not that which is to be,
   Watch you about the tomb,
   For the immortal bloom?

Search for your flowers in the celestial grove,
Look for your precious stream of human love
In the unfathomable sea above;
 Follow your missing bird,
 Where songs are always heard!

NEARER HOME.

One sweetly solemn thought
  Comes to me o'er and o'er;
I am nearer home to-day
  Than I ever have been before;

Nearer my Father's house,
  Where the many mansions be;
Nearer the great white throne,
  Nearer the crystal sea;

Nearer the bound of life,
  Where we lay our burdens down;
Nearer leaving the cross,
  Nearer gaining the crown!

But lying darkly between,
  Winding down through the night,
Is the silent, unknown stream,
  That leads at last to the light.

Closer and closer my steps
  Come to the dread abysm:
Closer Death to my lips
  Presses the awful chrism.

Oh, if my mortal feet
  Have almost gained the brink ;
If it be I am nearer home
  Even to-day than I think :

Father, perfect my trust ;
  Let my spirit feel in death,
That her feet are firmly set
  On the rock of a living faith !

4

MARCH CROCUSES.

O FICKLE and uncertain March,
  How could you have the heart,
To make the tender crocuses
  From their beds untimely start?

Those foolish, unsuspecting flowers,
  Too credulous to see,
That the sweetest promises of March
  Are not May's certainty.

When you smiled a few short hours ago,
  What said your whisper, light,
That made them lift their pretty heads
  So hopeful and so bright?

I could not catch a single word,
  But I saw your light caress;
And heard your rough voice softened down
  To a lover's tenderness.

O cruel and perfidious month,
  It makes me sick and sad,
To think how yesterday your smile
  Made all the blossoms glad!

O trustful, unsuspecting flowers,
  It breaks my heart to know,
That all your golden heads to-day
  Are underneath the snow!

THE SPIRITUAL BODY.

I HAVE a heavenly home,
To which my soul may come,
And where forever safe it may abide ;
Firmly and sure it stands,
That house not made with hands,
And garnished as a chamber for a bride!

'T is such as angels use,
Such as good men would choose ;
It hath all fair and pleasant things in sight:
Its walls as white and fine
As polished ivory shine,
And through its windows comes celestial light.

'T is builded fair and good,
In the similitude
Of the most royal palace of a king ;
And sorrow may not come
Into that heavenly home,
Nor pain, nor death, nor any evil thing.

Near it that stream doth pass
Whose waters, clear as glass,
Make glad the city of our God with song ;

Whose banks are fair as those
Whereon stray milk-white does,
Feeding among the lilies all day long.

And friends who once were here
Abide in dwellings near;
They went up thither on a heavenly road;
While I, though warned to go,
Yet linger here below,
Clinging to a most miserable abode.

The evil blasts drive in
Through chinks, which time and sin
Have battered in my wretched house of clay;
Yet in so vile a place,
Poor, unadorned with grace
I choose to live, or rather choose to stay.

And here I make my moan
About the days now gone,
About the souls passed on to their reward:
The souls that now have come
Into a better home,
And sit in heavenly places with their Lord.

'T is strange that I should cling
To this despisèd thing,
To this poor dwelling crumbling round my
    head;

Making myself content
In a low tenement
After my joys and friends alike are fled!

Yet I shall not, I know,
Be ready hence to go,
And dwell in my good palace, fair and whole,
Till unrelenting Death
Blows with his icy breath,
Upon my naked and unsheltered soul!

FAVORED.

Upon her cheek such color glows,
   And in her eye such light appears,
As comes, and only comes to those,
   Whose hearts are all untouched by years.

Yet half her wealth she doth not see,
   Nor half the kindness Heaven hath shown,
She never felt the poverty
   Of souls less favored than her own.

When all is hers that life can give,
   How can she tell how drear it seems
To those, uncomforted, who live
   In dreaming of their vanished dreams.

Supplied beyond her greatest need
   With lavish hoard of love and trust,
How shall she pity such as feed
   On hearts that years have turned to dust?

When sighs are smothered down, and lost
   In tenderest kisses ere they start,
What knows she of the bitter cost
   Of hiding sorrow in the heart?

While fondest care each wish supplies,
　　And heart-strings for her frowning break,
What can she know of one who dies
　　For love she scarcely deigns to take?

What should she know? No weak complaint,
　　No cry of pain should come to her,
If mine were all the woes I paint,
　　And she could be my comforter!

GRACIE.

GRACIE rises with a light
  In her clear face like the sun,
  Like the regal crownèd sun
That at morning meets her sight:
  Mirthful, merry little one,
  Happy, hopeful little one;
What has made her day so bright?

Who her sweet thoughts shall divine,
  As she draweth water up,
  Water from the well-spring up?
What hath made the draught so fine,
  That she drinketh of the cup,
  Of the dewy, dripping cup,
As if tasting royal wine?

Tripping up and down the stair,
  Hers are pleasant tasks to-day,
  Hers are easy tasks to-day;
Done without a thought of care,
  Something makes her work but play,
  All her work delightful play,
And the time a holiday.

And her lips make melody,
   Like a silver-singing rill,
   Like a laughing, leaping rill:
Then she breaks off suddenly;
   But her heart seems singing still,
   Beating out its music still,
Though it beateth silently.

And I wonder what she thinks;
   Only to herself she speaks,
   Very low and soft she speaks.
As she plants the scarlet pinks,
   Something plants them in her cheeks,
   Sets them blushing in her cheeks.
How I wonder what she thinks!

To a bruisèd vine she goes;
   Tenderly she does her part,
   Carefully she does her part,
As if, while she bound the rose,
   She were binding up a heart,
   Binding up a broken heart.
Doth she think but of the rose?

Bringing odorous leaf and flower
   To her bird she comes elate,
   Comes as one, with step elate,
Cometh in a happy hour
   To a true and tender mate.

Doth she think of such a mate ?
Is she trimming cage and bower?

How she loves the flower she brings !
 See her press her lips to this,
 Press her rosy mouth to this,
In a kiss that clings and clings.
 Hath the maiden learned that kiss,
 Learned that lingering, loving kiss,
From such cold insensate things?

What has changed our pretty one?
 A new light is in her eyes,
 In her downcast, drooping eyes,
As she walks beneath the moon.
 What has waked those piteous sighs,
 Waked her touching, tender sighs?
Has love found her out so soon ?

Even her mother wonderingly
 Saith : " How strange our darling seems,
 How unlike herself she seems."
And I answer: " Oft we see
 Women living as in dreams,
 When love comes into their dreams.
What if hers such dreaming be?"

But she says, undoubtingly :
 " Whatsoever else it mean,

This it surely cannot mean.
Gracie is a babe to me,
   Just a child of scarce sixteen,
   And it seems but yestere'en
That she sat upon my knee."

Ah wise mother! if you proved
   Lover never crossed her way,
   I would think the self-same way.
Ever since the world has moved,
   Babes seemed women in a day;
   And, alas! and well-a-day!
Men have wooed and maidens loved!

POOR MARGARET.

WE always called her "poor Margaret,"
  And spoke about her in mournful phrase;
And so she comes to my memory yet
  As she seemed to me in my childish days.

For in that which changing, waxeth old,
  In things which perish, we saw her poor,
But we never saw the wealth untold,
  She kept where treasures alone endure.

We saw her wrinkled, and pale, and thin,
  And bowed with toil, but we could not see
That her patient spirit grew straight within,
  In the power of its upright purity.

Over and over, every day,
  Bleaching her linen in sun and rain,
We saw her turn it until it lay
  As white on the grass as the snow had lain;

But we could not see how her Father's smile,
  Shining over her spirit there,
Was whitening for her all the while
  The spotless raiment His people wear.

She crimped and folded, smooth and nice,
  All our sister's clothes, when she came to
    wed, —
(Alas! that she only wore them twice,
  Once when living, and once when dead!)

And we said, she can have no wedding-day;
  Speaking sorrowfully, under our breath;
While her thoughts were all where they give
    away
No brides to lovers, and none to death.

Poor Margaret! she sleeps now under the sod,
  And the ills of her mortal life are past;
But heir with her Saviour, and heir of God,
  She is rich in her Father's House at last.

EARTH TO EARTH.

His hands with earthly work are done,
   His feet are done with roving;
We bring him now to thee and ask,
   The loved to take the loving.

Part back thy mantle, fringed with green,
   Broidered with leaf and blossom,
And lay him tenderly to sleep,
   Dear Earth, upon thy bosom.

Thy cheerful birds, thy liberal flowers,
   Thy woods and waters only
Gave him their sweet companionship
   And made his hours less lonely.

Though friendship never blest his way,
   And love denied her blisses;
No flower concealed her face from him,
   No wind withheld her kisses.

Nor man hath sighed, nor woman wept
   To go their ways without him;
So, lying here, he still will have
   His truest friends about him.

Then part thy mantle, fringed with green,
    Broidered with leaf and blossom,
And lay him tenderly to sleep,
    Dear Earth. upon thy bosom!

WOMEN.

'T is a sad truth, yet 't is a truth
  That does not need the proving:
They give their hearts away, unasked,
  And are not loved for loving.

Striving to win a little back,
  For all they feel they hide it;
And lips that tremble with their love,
  In trembling have denied it.

Sometimes they deem the kiss and smile
  Is life and love's beginning;
While he who wins the heart away,
  Is satisfied with winning.

Sometimes they think they have not found
  The right one for their mating;
And go on till the hair is white,
  And eyes are blind with waiting.

And if the mortal tarry still,
  They fill their lamps, undying;
And till the midnight wait to hear
  The " Heavenly Bridegroom " crying.

5

For while she lives, the best of them
  Is less a saint than woman;
And when her lips ask love divine,
  Her heart asks love that's human!

LADY MARJORY.

The Lady Marjory lay on her bed,
  Though the clock had struck the hour of
      noon,
And her cheek on the pillow burned as red
  As the bleeding heart of a rose in June ;
Like the shimmer and gleam of a golden mist
  Shone her yellow hair in the chamber dim ;
And a fairer hand was never kissed
  Than hers, with its fingers white and slim.

She spake to her women, suddenly, —
  "I have lain here long enough," she said ;
"Lain here a year, by night and day,
  And I hate the pillow, and hate the bed.
So carry me where I used to sit,
  I am not much for your arms to hold ;
Strange phantoms now through my fancy flit,
  And my head is hot and my feet are cold !"

They sat her up once more in her chair,
  And Alice, behind her, grew pale with dread
As she combed and combed her lady's hair,
  For the fever never left her head.

And before her, Rose on a humble seat
　Sat, but her young face wore no smile,
As she held in her lap her mistress' feet
　And chafed them tenderly all the while.

"Once I saw," said the lady, "a saintly nun,
　Who turned from the world and its pleasures
　　vain; —
When they clipped her tresses, one by one,
　How it must have eased her aching brain!
If it ached and burned as mine does now,
　And they cooled it thus, it was worth the
　　price; —
Good Alice, lay your hand on my brow,
　For my head is fire and my feet are ice!"

So the patient Alice stood in her place
　For hours behind her mistress' chair,
Bathing her fevered brow and face,
　Parting and combing her golden hair:
And Rose, whose cheek belied her name,
　Sitting before her, awed and still,
Kept at her hopeless task the same
　Till she felt, through all her frame, the chill.

"How my thoughts," the Lady Marjory said,
　"Go slipping into the past once more;
As the beads we are stringing slide down a
　　thread,
　When we drop the end along the floor:

Only a moment past, they slid
    Thus into the old time, dim and sweet;
I was where the honeysuckles hid
    My head and the daisies hid my feet.
I heard my Philip's step again,
    I felt the thrill of his kiss on my brow;
Ah! my cheek was not so crimson then,
    Nor my feet in the daisies cold as now!

" Dizzily still my senses swim,
    I am far away in a fairy land;
To the night when first I danced with him,
    And felt his look, as he touched my hand ;
Then my cheeks were bright with the flush
        and glow
    Of the joy that made the hours so fleet;
And my feet were rosy with warmth I know,
    As time to the music they lightly beat.

" 'T is strange how the things I remember, seem
    Blended together, and nothing plain ;
A dream is like truth, and truth like a dream,
    With this terrible fever in my brain.
But of all the visions that ever I had
    There is one returns to plague me most;
If it were not false it would drive me mad,
    Haunting me thus, like an evil ghost.

" It came to me first a year ago,
    Though I never have told a soul before,

But I dreamed, in the dead of the night, you
    know,
  That under the vines beside the door,
I watched for a step I did not hear,
  Stayed for a kiss I did not feel;
But I heard a something hiss in my ear
  Words that I shudder still to reveal.
I made no sound, and I gave no start,
  But I stood as the dead on the sea-floor stand,
While the demon's words fell slow on my heart
  As burning drops from a torturer's hand.

"'*Your Philip* stays.' it said, 'to-night,
  Where dark eyes hold him with magic spell;
Eyes from the stars that caught their light,
  Not from some pretty blue flower's bell!
With raven tresses he waits to play,
  They have bound him fast as a bird in a
    snare,
Did you think to hold him more than a day
  In the feeble mesh of your yellow hair?

"'Flowers or pearls in your tresses twist,
  As your fancy suits you, smile or sigh;
Or give your dainty hand to be kissed
  By other lips, and he will not die:
Hide your eyes in the veil of a nun,
  Weep till the rose in your cheek is dim;
Or turn to any beneath the sun,
  Henceforth it is all the same to him!'

"This was before I took my bed; —
Do you think a dream could make me ill;
Could put a fever in my head,
And touch my feet with an icy chill?
Yet I've hardly been myself I know
At times since then. for before my eyes
The wildest visions come and go,
Full of all wicked and cruel lies.

"Once the peal of marriage-bells, without,
Fell, or seemed to fall on my ear;
And I thought you went, and softly shut
The window, so that I might not hear;
That you turned from my eager look away,
And sadly bent your eyes on the ground,
As if you said, 'tis his wedding-day,
And her heart will break if she hears the
sound.

"And dreaming once, I dreamed I woke,
And heard you whisper, close at hand,
Men said. Sir Philip's heart was broke,
Since he gave himself for his wife's broad
land;
That he smiled on none, but frowned instead,
As he stalked through his halls, like a ghost
forlorn;
And the nurse who had held him, a baby, said,
He had better have died in the day he was
born!"

So, till the low sun, fading, cast
    Across her chamber his dying beams,
The Lady Marjory lived in the past,
    Telling her women of all her dreams.
Then she changed; — " I am almost well," she
      said,
    " I feel so strangely free from pain;
Oh, if only the fever would leave my head,
    And if only my feet were warm again !
And something whispers me, clear and low,
    I shall soon be done with lying there,
So to-morrow, when I am better, you know,
    You must come, good Alice, and dress my
      hair.

" We will give Sir Philip a glad surprise,
    He will come, I know, at morn or night ;
And I want the help of your hands and eyes
    To dress me daintily all in white ;
Bring snowy lilies for my hair ; —
    And, Rose, when all the rest is done,
Take from my satin slippers the pair
    That are softest and whitest, and put them on.
But take me to bed now, where in the past
    You have placed me many a time and oft ;
I am so tired, I think at last
    I shall sleep, if the pillow is cool and soft."

So the patient Alice took her head,
    And the sweet Rose took her mistress' feet,

And they laid her tenderly on the bed,
　And smoothed the pillow, and smoothed the
　　sheet.
Then she wearily closed her eyes, they say,
　On this world, with all its sorrow and sin;
And her head and her heart at the break of
　　day,
　Were as cold as ever her feet had been!

THE OLD MAN'S DARLING.

So I'm "crazy," in loving a man of three-score;
Why, I never had come to my senses before,
But I'm doubtful of yours, if your're thinking
  to prove
My insanity, just by the fact of my love.

You would like to know what are his wonder-
  ful wiles?
Only delicate praises, and flattering smiles!
'T is no spell of enchantment, no magical art,
But the way he says "darling," that goes to
  my heart.

Yes, he's "sixty," I cannot dispute with you
  there,
But you'd make him a hundred, I think, if you
  dare;
And I'm glad all his folly of first love is past,
Since I'm sure, of the two, it is best to be last.

"His hair is as white as the snow-drift," you
  say;
Then I never shall see it change slowly to gray;

But I almost could wish, for his dear sake alone,
That my tresses were nearer the hue of his own.

" He can't see ; " then I 'll help him to see and
  to hear,
If it 's needful, you know, I can sit very near ;
And he 's young enough yet to interpret the
  tone
Of a heart that is beating up close to his own.

I " must aid him ; " ah ! that is my pleasure
  and pride,
I should love him for this if for nothing beside ;
And though I 've more reasons than I can recall,
Yet the one that " he needs me " is strongest
  of all.

So, if I 'm insane, you will own, I am sure,
That the case is so hopeless it 's past any cure ;
And, besides, it is acting no very wise part,
To be treating the head for disease of the
  heart.

And if any thing could make a woman believe
That no dream can delude, and no fancy de-
  ceive ;
That she never knew lover's enchantment be·
  fore,
It 's being the darling of one of three-score !

THE UNHONORED.

Alas, alas! how many sighs
Are breathed for his sad fate, who dies
With triumph dawning on his eyes.

What thousands for the soldier weep,
From his first battle gone to sleep
That slumber which is long and deep.

But who about his fate can tell,
Who struggled manfully and well;
Yet fainted on the march, and fell?

Or who above his rest makes moan,
Who dies in the sick-tent alone —
" Only a private, name unknown ! "

What tears down Pity's cheek have run
For poets singing in the sun,
Stopped suddenly, their song half done.

But for the hosts of souls below,
Who to eternal silence go,
Hiding their great unspoken woe;

Who sees amid their ranks go down,
Heroes, that never won renown,
And martyrs, with no martyr's crown?

Unrecognized, a poet slips
Into death's total, long eclipse,
With breaking heart, and wordless lips;

And never any brother true
Utters the praise that was his due —
"This man was greater than ye knew!"

No maiden by his grave appears,
Crying out in long after years,
"I would have loved him," through her tears.

We weep for her, untimely dead,
Who would have pressed the marriage-bed,
Yet to Death's chamber went instead.

But who deplores the sadder fate,
Of her who finds no mortal mate,
And lives and dies most desolate?

Alas! 't is sorrowful to know
That she who finds least love below,
Finds least of pity for her woe.

Hard is her fate who feels life past,
When loving hands still hold her fast,
And loving eyes watch to the last.

But she, whose lids no kisses prest,
Who crossed her own hands on her breast,
And went to her eternal rest;

She had so sad a lot below,
That her unutterable woe
Only the pitying God can know!

When little hands are dropped away
From the warm bosom where they lay,
And the poor mother holds but clay;

What human lip that does not moan,
What heart that does not inly groan,
And make such suffering its own?

Yet, sitting mute in their despair,
With their unnoticed griefs to bear,
Are childless women everywhere;

Who never knew, nor understood,
That which is woman's greatest good,
The sacredness of motherhood.

But putting down their hopes and fears,
Claiming no pity and no tears,
They live the measure of their years.

They see age stealing on apace,
And put the gray hairs from their face,
No children's fingers shall displace!

Though grief hath many a form and show,
I think that unloved women know
The very bottom of life's woe!

And that the God, who pitying sees,
Hath yet a recompense for these,
Kept in the long eternities!

THE ONLY ORNAMENT.

EVEN as a child too well she knew
   Her lack of loveliness and grace;
So, like an unprized weed she grew,
   Grudging the meanest flower its face.

Often with tears her sad eyes filled,
   Watching the plainest birds that went
About her home to pair, and build
   Their humble nests in sweet content.

No melody was in her words;
   You thought her, as she passed along,
As brown and homely as the birds
   She envied, but without their song.

She saw, and sighed to see how glad
   Earth makes her fair and favored child;
While all the beauty that she had
   Was in her smile, nor oft she smiled.

So seasons passed her and were gone,
   She musing by herself apart;
Till the vague longing that is known
   To woman came into her heart.

That feeling born when fancy teems
  With all that makes this life a good,
Came to her, with its wondrous dreams,
  That bless and trouble maidenhood.

She would have deemed it joy to sit
  In any home, or great or small,
Could she have hoped to brighten it
  For one who thought of her at all.

At night, or in some secret place,
  She used to think, with tender pain,
How infants love the mother's face,
  And know not if 't is fair or plain.

She longed to feast her hungry eyes
  On any thing her own could please;
To sing soft, loving, lullabies
  To children lying on her knees.

And yet beyond the world she went,
  Unmissed, as if she had not been,
Taking her only ornament,
  A meek and quiet soul within.

None ever knew her heart was pained,
  Or that she grieved to live unsought;
They deemed her cold and self-contained,
  Contented in her realm of thought.

Her patient life, when it was o'er,
   Was one that all the world approved;
Some marvelled at, some pitied her,
   But neither man nor woman loved.

Even little children felt the same;
   Were shy of her, from awe or fear; —
I wonder if she knew they came,
   And scattered roses on her bier!

JOHN BROWN.

MEN silenced on his faithful lips
    Words of resistless truth and power; —
Those words, reëchoing now, have made
    The gathering war-cry of the hour.

They thought to darken down in blood
    The light of freedom's burning rays;
The beacon-fires we tend to-day
    Were lit in that undying blaze.

They took the earthly prop and staff
    Out of an unresisting hand;
God came, and led him safely on,
    By ways they could not understand.

They knew not, when from his old eyes
    They shut the world for evermore,
The ladder by which angels come
    Rests firmly on the dungeon's floor.

They deemed no vision bright could cheer
    His stony couch and prison ward;
He slept to dream of Heaven, and rose
    To build a Bethel to the Lord!

They showed to his unshrinking gaze
  The "sentence" men have paled to see;
He read God's writing of "reprieve,"
  And grant of endless liberty.

They tried to conquer and subdue
  By marshalled power and bitter hate;
The simple manhood of the man
  Was braver that an armèd State.

They hoped at last to make him feel
  The felon's shame, and felon's dread;
And lo! the martyr's crown of joy
  Settled forever on his head!

GARIBALDI IN PIEDMONT.

HEMMED in by the hosts of the Austrians,
　　No succor at hand,
Adown the green passes of Piedmont,
　　That beautiful land,
　　Moves a patriot band.

Two long days and nights, watchful, sleepless,
　　Have they ridden, nor yet
Checked the rein, though the feet of their horses,
　　In the ripe vineyard set,
　　By its wine have been wet.

What know they of weariness, hunger,
　　What good can they lack,
While they follow their brave Garibaldi,
　　Who never turns back,
　　Never halts on his track?

By the Austrians outnumbered, surrounded,
　　On left and on right;
Strong and fearless he moves as a giant,
　　Who rouses to fight
　　From the slumbers of night.

So, over the paths of Orfano,
    His brave horseman tread,
Long after the sun, halting wearied,
    Hath hidden his head
    In his tent-folds of red.

Every man with his eye on his leader,
    Whom a spell must have bound,
For he rideth as still as the shadow,
    That keeps step on the ground,
    In a silence profound.

With the harmony Nature is breathing,
    His soul is in tune ;
He is bathed in a bath of the splendor
    Of the beautiful moon,
    Of the air soft as June!

But what sound meets the ear of the soldier ;
    What menacing tone?
For look! how the horse and the rider
    Have suddenly grown
    As if carvèd in stone.

Leaning down toward that fair grove of olives
    He waits; doth it mean
That he catches the tramp of the Austrians,
    That his quick eye hath seen
    Their bayonets' sheen?

Nay! there, where the thick leaves about her
    By the music are stirred,
Sits a nightingale singing her rapture,
    And the hero hath heard
    But the voice of a bird!

A hero! ay, more than a hero
    By this he appears;
A man, with a heart that is tender,
    Unhardened by years;
    Who shall tell what he hears?

Not the voice of the nightingale only,
    Floating soft on the breeze,
But the music of dear human voices,
    And blended with these
    The sound of the seas.

Ah, the sea, the dear sea! from the cradle
    She took him to rest;
Leaping out from the arms of his mother,
    He went to her breast
    And was softly caressed.

Perchance he is back on her bosom,
    Safe from fear or alarms,
Clasping close as of old that first mistress
    Whose wonderful charms
    Drew him down to her arms.

By the memories that come with that singing
　　His soul has been wiled
Far away from the danger of battle;
　　Transported, beguiled,
　　He again is a child,

Sitting down at the feet of the mother,
　　Whose prayers are the charm
That ever in conflict and peril
　　Has strengthened his arm,
　　And kept him from harm.

Nay, who knows but his spirit that moment
　　Was gone in its quest
Of that bright bird of paradise, vanished
　　Too soon from the nest
　　Where her lover was blest!

For unerring the soul finds its kindred,
　　Below or above;
And, as over the great waste of waters
　　To her mate goes the dove,
　　So love seeks its love.

Did he see her first blush, burning softly
　　His kisses beneath;
Or her dear look of love, when he held her
　　Disputing with Death
　　For the last precious breath?

Lost Anita! sweet vision of beauty,
    Too sacred to tell
Is the tale of her dear life, that, hidden
    In his heart's deepest cell,
    Is kept safely and well.

And what matter his dreams! He whose bosom
    With such rapture can glow
Hath something within him more sacred
    Than the hero may show,
    Or the patriot know.

And this praise, for man or for hero,
    The best were, in sooth ;
His heart, through life's conflict and peril,
    Has kept its first truth,
    And the dreams of its youth.

DOVES' EYES.

THERE are eyes that look through us,
    With the power to undo us.
Eyes of the lovingest, tenderest blue,
Clear as the heavens and as truthful too;
    But these are not my love's eyes,
    For, behold, he hath doves' eyes!

    There are eyes half defiant,
    Half meek and compliant;
Black eyes, with a wondrous, witching charm,
To bring us good or to work us harm;
    But these are not my love's eyes,
    For, behold, he hath doves' eyes!

    There are eyes to our feeling
    Forever appealing;
Eyes of a helpless, pleading brown,
That into our very souls look down;
    But these are not my love's eyes,
    For, behold, he hath doves' eyes!

    O eyes, dearest, sweetest,
    In beauty completest;

Whose perfectness cannot be told in a word, —
Clear and deep as the eyes of a soft, brooding
    bird ;
    These, these, are my love's eyes,
    For, behold, he hath doves' eyes !

EQUALITY.

Most favored lady in the land,
　　I well can bear your scorn or pride ;
For in all truest wealth, to-day,
　　I stand an equal by your side!

No better parentage have you, —
　　One is our Father, one our Friend ;
The same inheritance awaits
　　Our claiming, at the journey's end.

No broader flight your thought can take, —
　　Faith on no firmer basis rest;
Nor can the dreams of fancy wake
　　A sweeter tumult in your breast.

Life may to you bring every good,
　　Which from a Father's hand can fall;
But if true lips have said to me,
　　"I love you," I have known it all !

HOMESICK.

Comfort me with apples!
I am sick unto death, I am sad to despair;
My trouble is more than my strength is to bear;
Back again to the green hills that first met my
 sight
I come, as a child to its mother, to-night; —
 Comfort me with apples!

Comfort me with apples!
Bring the ripe mellow fruit from the early
 " sweet bough," —
(Is the tree that we used to climb growing there
 now ?)
And " russets," whose cheeks are as freckled
 and dun
As the cheeks of the children that play in the
 sun ; —
 Comfort me with apples!

Comfort me with apples!
Gather those streaked with red, that we named
 " morning-light."
Our good father set, when his hair had grown
 white,

The tree, though he said, when he planted the
    root,
" The hands of another shall gather the
    fruit ; " —
    Comfort me with apples !

    Comfort me with apples !
Go down to the end of the orchard, and bring
The fair " lady-fingers," that grew by the spring ;
Pale " bell-flowers," and " pippins," all burnished
    with gold,
Like the fruit the Hesperides guarded of old ; —
    Comfort me with apples !

    Comfort me with apples !
Get the sweet "junietta," so loved by the
    bees,
And the " pearmain," that grew on the queen
    of the trees ;
And close by the brook, where they hang ripe
    and lush,
Go and shake down the best of them all, —
    " maiden's-blush ; " —
    Comfort me with apples !

    Comfort me with apples !
For lo ! I am sick ; I am sad and opprest ;
I come back to the place where, a child, I was
    blest.

Hope is false, love is vain, for the old things I
    sigh;
And if these cannot comfort me, then I must
    die!
      Comfort me with apples!

EBB-TIDE.

With her white face full of agony,
  Under her dripping locks,
I hear the wretched, restless sea,
  Complaining to the rocks.

Helplessly in her great despair,
  She shudders on the sand,
The bright weeds dropping from her hair,
  And the pale shells from her hand.

'T is pitiful thus to see her lie,
  With her beating, heaving breast,
Here, where she fell, when cast aside,
  Sobbing herself to rest.

Alas, alas! for the foolish sea,
  Why was there none to say:
The wave that strikes on the heartless stone
  Must break and fall away?

Why could she not have known that this
  Would be her fate at length; —
For the hand, unheld, must slip at last,
  Though it cling with love's own strength?

"FIELD PREACHING."

I HAVE been out to-day in field and wood,
Listening to praises sweet and counsel good
Such as a little child had understood,
       That, in its tender youth,
Discerns the simple eloquence of truth.

The modest blossoms, crowding round my way,
Though they had nothing great or grand to say,
Gave out their fragrance to the wind all day;
       Because His loving breath,
With soft persistence, won them back from
    death.

And the right royal lily, putting on
Her robes, more rich than those of Solomon,
Opened her gorgeous missal in the sun,
       And thanked Him, soft and low,
Whose gracious, liberal hand had clothed her so.

When wearied, on the meadow-grass I sank;
So narrow was the rill from which I drank,
An infant might have stepped from bank to
    bank;

7

And the tall rushes near
Lapping together, hid its waters clear.

Yet to the ocean joyously it went;
And rippling in the fullness of content,
Watered the pretty flowers that o'er it leant;
For all the banks were spread
With delicate flowers that on its bounty fed.

The stately maize, a fair and goodly sight,
With serried spear-points bristling sharp and
bright,
Shook out his yellow tresses, for delight,
To all their tawny length,
Like Samson, glorying in his lusty strength.

And every little bird upon the tree,
Ruffling his plumage bright, for ecstacy,
Sang in the wild insanity of glee;
And seemed, in the same lays,
Calling his mate and uttering songs of praise.

The golden grasshopper did chirp and sing;
The plain bee, busy with her housekeeping,
Kept humming cheerfully upon the wing,
As if she understood
That, with contentment, labor was a good.

I saw each creature, in his own best place,
To the Creator lift a smiling face,

Praising continually His wondrous grace ;
                As if the best of all
Life's countless blessings was to live at all !

So with a book of sermons, plain and true,
Hid in my heart, where I might turn them
        through,
I went home softly, through the falling dew,
                Still listening, rapt and calm,
To Nature giving out her evening psalm.

While, far along the west, mine eyes discerned,
Where, lit by God, the fires of sunset burned,
The tree-tops, unconsumed, to flame were
        turned ;
                And I, in that great hush,
Talked with His angels in each burning bush !

HAPPY WOMEN.

Impatient women, as you wait
 In cheerful homes to-night, to hear
The sound of steps that, soon or late,
 Shall come as music to your ear;

Forget yourselves a little while,
 And think in pity of the pain
Of women who will never smile
 To hear a coming step again.

With babes that in their cradle sleep,
 Or cling to you in perfect trust;
Think of the mothers left to weep,
 Their babies lying in the dust.

And when the step you wait for comes,
 And all your world is full of light,
O women, safe in happy homes,
 Pray for all lonesome souls to-night!

HYMN.

How dare I in thy courts appear,
  Or raise to thee my voice?
I only serve thee, Lord, with fear,
  With trembling I rejoice.

I have not all forgot thy word,
  Nor wholly gone astray;
I follow thee, but O my Lord,
  So faint, so far away!

That thou wilt pardon and receive
  Of sinners even the chief,
Lord, I believe, — Lord, I believe;
  Help thou mine unbelief!

GATHERING BLACKBERRIES.

LITTLE Daisy smiling wakes
From her sleep as morning breaks,
    Why, she knoweth well;
Yet if you should ask her, surely
She would answer you demurely,
    That she cannot tell.

Careful Daisy, with no sound,
Slips her white feet to the ground,
    Saying, very low,
She must rise and help her mother,
And be ready, if her brother
    Needs her aid, to go!

Foolish Daisy, o'er her lips
Only that poor falsehood slips,
    Truth is in her cheeks;
Her own words cannot deceive her,
Her own heart will not believe her,
    In a blush it speaks.

Daisy knows that, when the heat
Dries the dew upon the wheat,
    She will be away;

She and Ernest, just another
Who, she says, is like a brother,
    Making holiday.

For the blackberries to-day
Will be ripe, the reapers say,
    Ripe as they can be ;
And not wholly for the pleasure,
But lest others find the treasure,
    She must go and see.

Eager Daisy, at the gate
Meeting Ernest, scarce can wait,
    But she checks her heart ;
And she says, her soft eyes beaming
With an innocent, grave seeming ;
    " Is it time to start ? "

Cunning Daisy tries to go
Very womanly and slow,
    And to act so well
That, if any one had seen them,
With the dusty road between them,
    What was there to tell ?

Happy Daisy, when they gain
The green windings of the lane,
    Where the hedge is thick ;
For they find, beneath its shadow,

Wild sweet roses in the meadow,
　　More than they can pick.

Bending low, and rising higher,
Scarlet pinks their lamps of fire
　　Lightly swing about ;
And the wind that blows them over
Out of sight among the clover,
　　Seems to blow them out !

Doubting Daisy, as she hies
Toward the field of berries, cries :
　　" What if they be red ? "
Black and ripe they find them rather,
Black and ripe enough to gather,
　　As the reapers said.

Lucky Daisy, Ernest finds
Berries for her in the vines,
　　Hidden where she stands ;
And with fearless arm he pushes
Back the cruel, briery bushes,
　　That would hurt her hands.

He would have her hold her cup
Just for him to fill it up,
　　But away she trips ;
Picking daintily, she lingers
Till she dyes her pretty fingers
　　Redder than her lips.

Thoughtful Daisy, what she hears,
What she hopes, or what she fears,
    Who of us can tell?.
For if, going home, she carries
Richer treasure than her berries,
    She will guard it well!

Puzzled Daisy does not know
Why the sun, who rises slow,
    Hurries overhead;
He, that lingered at the morning,
Drops at night with scarce a warning
    On his cloudy bed.

All too narrow at the start
Seemed the path, they kept apart,
    Though the way was rough;
Now the path, that through the hollow
Closely side by side they follow,
    Seemeth wide enough.

Hopeful Daisy, will the days
That are brightening to her gaze
    Brighter grow than this?
Will she, mornings without number,
Wake up restless from her slumber,
    Just for happiness?

Will the friend so kind to-day,
Always push the thorns away,

With which earth is rife?
Will he be her true, true lover,
Will he make her cup run over
   With the wine of life?

Blessèd Daisy, will she be,
If above mortality
   Thus she stands apart;
Cursèd, if the hand, unsparing,
Let the thorns fly backward, tearing
   All her bleeding heart!

Periled Daisy, none can know
What the future has to show;
   There must come what must;
But, if blessings be forbidden,
Let the truth awhile be hidden —
   Let her hope and trust.

Let all women born to weep,
Their heart's breaking — all who keep
   Hearts still young and whole,
Pray, as fearing no denying,
Pray with me, as for the dying,
   For this maiden's soul!

A TENT SCENE.

OUR generals sat in their tent one night,
  On the Mississippi's banks,
Where Vicksburg sullenly still held out
  Against the assaulting ranks.

They could hear the firing as they talked,
  Long after set of sun ;
And the blended noise of a thousand guns
  In the distance seemed as one.

All at once Sherman started to his feet,
  And listened to the roar,
His practiced ear had caught a sound,
  That he had not heard before.

" They have mounted another gun on the walls ;
  'T is new," he said, " I know ;
I can tell the voice of a gun, as a man
  Can tell the voice of his foe !

" What ! not a soul of you hears but me ?
  No matter, I am right ;
Bring me my horse ! I must silence this
  Before I sleep to-night ! "

He was gone; and they listened to the ring
  Of hoofs on the distant track;
Then talked and wondered for a while, —
  In an hour he was back.

" Well, General! what is the news ? " they cried,
  As he entered flushed and worn ;
" We have picked their gunners off, and the gun
  Will be dislodged at morn ! "

LOSS AND GAIN.

Life grows better every day,
  If we live in deed and truth;
So I am not used to grieve
  For the vanished joys of youth.

For though early hopes may die,
  Early dreams be rudely crossed;
Of the past we still can keep
  Treasures more than we have lost.

For if we but try to gain,
  Life's best good, and hold it fast,
We grow very rich in love
  Ere our mortal days are past.

Rich in golden stores of thought,
  Hopes that give us wealth untold;
Rich in all sweet memories,
  That grow dearer, growing old.

For when we have lived and loved,
  Tasted suffering and bliss,
All the common things of life
  Have been sanctified by this.

What my eyes behold to-day
　Of this good world is not all,
Earth and sky are crowded full
　Of the beauties they recall.

When I watch the sunset now,
　As its glories change and glow
I can see the light of suns
　That were faded long ago.

When I look up to the stars,
　I find burning overhead
All the stars that ever shone
　In the nights that now are dead.

And a loving, tender word,
　Dropping from the lips of truth,
Brings each dear remembered tone
　Echoing backward from my youth.

When I meet a human face,
　Lit for me with light divine,
I recall all loving eyes,
　That have ever answered mine.

Therefore, they who were my friends
　Never can be changed or old;
For the beauty of their youth
　Fond remembrance well can hold.

And even they whose feet here crossed
  O'er the noiseless calm abyss,
To the better shore which seemed
  Once so far away from this;

Are to me as dwelling now
  Just across a pleasant stream,
Over which they come and go,
  As we journey in a dream.

DRAWING WATER.

He had drunk from founts of pleasure,
   And his thirst returned again;
He had hewn out broken cisterns,
   And behold! his work was vain.

And he said, "Life is a desert,
   Hot, and measureless, and dry;
And God will not give me water,
   Though I strive, and faint, and die."

Then he heard a voice make answer,
   "Rise and roll the stone away;
Sweet and precious springs lie hidden
   In thy pathway every day."

And he said, his heart was sinful,
   Very sinful was his speech:
"All the cooling wells I thirst for
   Are too deep for me to reach."

But the voice cried, "Hope and labor;
   Doubt and idleness is death;
Shape a clear and goodly vessel,
   With the patient hands of faith."

So he wrought and shaped the vessel,
　Looked, and lo! a well was there;
And he drew up living water,
　With a golden chain of prayer.

8

TOO LATE.

Blessings, alas! unmerited,
Freely as evening dews are shed
Each day on my unworthy head.

So that my very sins but prove
The sinlessness of Him above
And His unutterable love.

And yet, as if no ear took heed,
Not what I ask, but what I need,
Comes down in answer, when I plead.

So that my heart with anguish cries,
My soul almost within me dies,
'Twixt what God gives, and what denies.

For howsoe'er with good it teems,
The life accomplished never seems
The blest fulfillment of its dreams.

Therefore, when nearest happiness,
I only say, The thing I miss —
That would have perfected my bliss!

When harvests great are mine to reap,
Too late, too late! I sit and weep,
My best-belovèd lies asleep!

Sometimes my griefs are hard to bear,
Sometimes my comforts I would share,
And the one dearest is not there.

That which is mine to-day, I know,
Had made a paradise below,
Only a little year ago.

The sunshine we then did crave,
As having almost power to save,
Keeps now the greenness of a grave.

To have our dear one safe from gloom,
We planned a fair and pleasant room,
And lo! Fate builded up a tomb.

An empty heart, with cries unstilled,
An empty house, with love unfilled,
These are the things our Father willed.

And bowing to Him, as we must,
Whose name is Love, whose way is just,
We have no refuge, but our trust.

LOVERS AND SWEETHEARTS.

FAIR youth, too timid to lift your eyes
    To the maiden with downcast look,
As you mingle the gold and brown of your
       curls
    Together over a book;
A fluttering hope that she dare not name
    Her trembling bosom heaves;
And your heart is thrilled, when your fingers
       meet,
    As you softly turn the leaves.

Perchance you two will walk alone
    Next year at some sweet day's close,
And your talk will fall to a tenderer tone,
    As you liken her cheek to a rose;
And then her face will flush and glow,
    With a hopeful, happy red;
Outblushing all the flowers that grow
    A-near in the garden-bed.

If you plead for hope, she may bashful drop
    Her head on your shoulder, low;
And you will be lovers and sweethearts then
    As youths and maidens go:

Lovers and sweethearts, dreaming dreams,
  And seeing visions that please,
With never a thought that life is made
  Of great realities ;

That the cords of love must be strong as death
  Which hold and keep a heart,
Not daisy-chains, that snap in the breeze,
  Or break with their weight apart;
For the pretty colors of youth's fair morn
  Fade out from the noonday sky;
And blushing loves, in the roses born,
  Alas ! with the roses die !

But the love, that when youth's morn is past,
  Still sweet and true survives,
Is the faith we need to lean upon
  In the crises of our lives ;
The love that shines in the eyes grown dim,
  In the voice that trembles speaks;
And sees the roses, that years ago
  Withered and died in our cheeks ;

That sheds a halo round us still,
  Of soft immortal light,
When we change youth's golden coronal
  For a crown of silver white :
A love for sickness and for health,
  For rapture and for tears;

That will live for us, and bear with us
  Through all our mortal years.

And such there is ; there are lovers here,
  On the brink of the grave that stand,
Who shall cross to the hills beyond, and walk
  Forever hand in hand !
Pray, youth and maid, that your end be theirs,
  Who are joined no more to part;
For death comes not to the living soul,
  Nor age to the loving heart !

THE ROSE.

THE sun, who smiles wherever he goes,
  Till the flowers all smile again,
Fell in love one day with a bashful rose,
  That had been a bud till then.

So he pushed back the folds of the soft green
    hood
  That covered her modest grace,
And kissed her as only the bold sun could,
  Till the crimson burned in her face.

But woe for the day when his golden hair
  Tangled her heart in a net;
And woe for the night of her dark despair,
  When her cheek with tears was wet!

For she loved him as only a young rose could ;
  And he left her crushed and weak,
Striving in vain with her faded hood
  To cover her burning cheek.

JENNIE.

You have sent me from her tomb
   A poor withered flower to keep,
Broken off in perfect bloom,
   Such as hers, who lies asleep —
Underneath the roses lies,
Hidden from your mortal eyes,
Never from your heart concealed,
Always to your soul revealed.

Oh, to think, as day and night
   Come and go, and go and come,
How the smile which was its light
   Hath been darkened in your home!
Oh, to think that those dear eyes,
Copied from the summer skies,
Could have veiled their heavenly blue
From the sunshine, and from you!

Oh. to have that tender mouth,
   With its loveliness complete,
Shut up in its budding youth
   From all kisses, fond and sweet!
Fairest blossom, red and rare,
Could not with her lips compare;

Yea, her mouth's young beauty shamed
All the roses ever named.

Why God hid her from your sight,
  Leaving anguish in her place,
At the noonday sent the night,
 'Night that almost hid His face,
Not to us is fully shown,
Not to mortals can be known,
Though they strive, through tears and doubt,
Still to guess His meaning out.

Full of mystery 'tis, and yet
  If you claspèd still those charms,
Mother, might you not forget
  Mothers who have empty arms?
If you satisfied in her
  Every want and every need,
Could you be a comforter
  To the hearts that moan and bleed?

Take this solace for your woe:
  God's love never groweth dim ;
All of goodness that you know,
  All your loving comes from Him !
You say, " She has gone to death ! "
Very tenderly, God saith:
" *Better so ; I make her mine,*
And my love exceedeth thine ! "

ARCHIE.

Oh to be back in the cool summer shadow
Of that old maple-tree down in the meadow;
Watching the smiles that grew dearer and
      dearer,
Listening to lips that drew nearer and nearer;
Oh to be back in the crimson-topped clover,
Sitting again with my Archie, my lover!

Oh for the time when I felt his caresses
Smoothing away from my forehead the tresses;
When up from my heart to my cheek went the
      blushes,
As he said that my voice was as sweet as the
      thrushes;
As he told me, my eyes were bewitchingly
      jetty,
And I answered, 't was only my love made
      them pretty!

Talk not of maiden reserve or of duty,
Or hide from my vision such visions of beauty;
Pulses above may beat calmly and even, —
We have been fashioned for earth, and not
      heaven :

Angels are perfect, I am but a woman ;
Saints may be passionless, Archie is human.

Say not that heaven hath tenderer blisses
To her on whose brow drops the soft rain of
        kisses ;
Preach not the promise of priests or evan-
        gels, —
Love-crowned, who asks for the crown of the
        angels ?
Yea, all that the wall of pure jasper incloses,
Takes not the sweetness from sweet bridal
        roses !

Tell me, that when all this life shall be over,
I shall still love him, and he be my lover;
That mid flowers more fragrant than clover or
        heather
My Archie and I shall be always together,
Loving eternally, met ne'er to sever,
Then you may tell me of heaven forever !

COWPER'S CONSOLATION.*

He knew what mortals know when tried
    By suffering's worst and last extreme;
He knew the ecstacy allied
            To bliss supreme.

Souls, hanging on his melody,
    Have caught his rapture of belief;
The heart of all humanity
            Has felt his grief.

In sweet compassion and in love
    Poets about his tomb have trod;
And softly hung their wreaths above
            The hallowed sod.

His hymns of victory, clear and strong,
    Over the hosts of sin and doubt,
Still make the Christian's battle-song,
           And triumph-shout.

* The most important events of Cowper's latter years were
audibly announced to him before they occurred. We find him
writing of Mrs. Unwin's "approaching and sudden death,"
when her health, although feeble, was not such as to occasion
alarm. His lucid intervals, and the return of his disorder,
were announced to him in the same remarkable manner. —
Cowper's *Audible Illusions*.

Tasting sometimes his Father's grace,
  Yet for wise purposes allowed
Seldom to see the " smiling face "
        Behind the cloud;

Surely when he was left the prey
  Of torments only Heaven can still,
" God moved in a mysterious way "
        To work His will.

Yet many a soul through life has trod
  Untroubled o'er securest ground,
Nor knew that " closer walk with God "
        His footsteps found.

With its great load of grief to bear,
  The reed, though bruisèd, might not break ;
God did not leave him to despair,
        Nor quite forsake.

The pillow by his tear-drops wet,
  The stoniest couch that heard his cries,
Had near a golden ladder set
        That touched the skies.

And at the morning on his bed,
  And in sweet visions of the night,
Angels, descending, comforted
        His soul with light.

Standing upon the hither side,
　How few of all the earthly host
Have signaled those whose feet have trod
　　　　The heavenly coast.

Yet his it was at times to see,
　In glimpses faint and half-revealed,
That strange and awful mystery
　　　　By death concealed.

And, as the glory thus discerned
　His heart desired, with strong desire;
By seraphs touched, his sad lips burned
　　　　With sacred fire.

As ravens to Elijah bare,
　At morn and eve, the promised bread;
So by the spirits of the air
　　　　His soul was fed.

And, even as the prophet rose
　Triumphant on the flames of love,
The fiery chariot of his woes
　　　　Bore him above.

Oh, shed no tears for such a lot,
　Nor deem he passed uncheered, alone;
He walked with God, and he was not,
　　　　God took his own!

A PRAYER.

I ASK not wealth, but power to take
  And use the things I have aright,
Not years, but wisdom that shall make
  My life a profit and delight.

I ask not, that for me, the plan
  Of good and ill be set aside ;
But that the common lot of man
  Be nobly borne, and glorified.

I know I may not always keep
  My steps in places green and sweet,
Nor find the pathway of the deep
  A path of safety for my feet ;

But pray, that when the tempest's breath
  Shall fiercely sweep my way about,
I make not shipwreck of my faith
  In the unbottomed sea of doubt :

And that, though it be mine to know
  How hard the stoniest pillow seems,
Good angels still may come and go,
  About the places of my dreams.

I do not ask for love below,
  That friends shall never be estranged;
But for the power of loving, so
  My heart may keep its youth unchanged.

Youth, joy, wealth — Fate I give thee these;
  Leave faith and hope till life is past;
And leave my heart's best impulses
  Fresh and unfailing to the last!

MEMORIAL.

Toiling early, and toiling late,
  Though her name was never heard,
To the least of her Saviour's little ones,
  She meekly ministered, —

Publishing good news to the poor ;
  She came to their homes unsought,
And her feet on the hills were beautiful,
  For the blessings which they brought.

Such a perfect life as hers, again,
  In the world we may not see ;
For her heart was full of love, and her hands
  Were full of charity.

Oh woe for us! cried the weak and poor,
  And the weary ones made moan ;
And the mourners went about the streets,
  When she went to her home alone.

And, seeing her go from the field of life,
  From toiling, early and late,
We said, What good has she gained, to show
  For a sacrifice so great?

9

We might have learned from the husbandman
  To wait more patiently,
Since his seed of wheat lies under the snow,
  Not quickened, except it die.

For when we raised our eyes again
  From their sorrow's wintry night,
We saw how the deeds of good she hid
  Were pushing up to the light.

And still the precious seed she sowed,
  In patient, sorrowing trust,
Though not for her mortal eyes to see,
  Comes blossoming out of the dust.

THE HUNTER'S WIFE.

My head is sick and my heart is faint,
I am wearied out with my own complaint,
    Answer me, come to me, then;
For, lo! I have pleaded by every thing
My brain could dream, or my lips could sing;
I have called you lover, 'and called you king,
    And man of the race of men!

Come to me glad, and I will be glad;
But if you are weary, or if you are sad,
    I will be patient and meek,
Nor word, nor smile will I seem to crave;
But I'll sit and wait, like an Eastern slave,
Or wife, in the lodge of an Indian brave,
    In silence, till you speak.

Come, for the power of life and death
Hangs for me on the lightest breath
    Of the lips that I believe;
Only pause by the cooling lake,
Till your weary mule her thirst shall slake;
'T were a fearful thing if a heart should break,
    And you held its sweet reprieve!

Sleep lightly under the loving moon ;
Rise with the morning, and ride till noon ;
 Ride till the stars are above!
And as you distance the mountain herds,
And shame the flight of the summer birds,
Say softly over the tenderest words
 The poets have sung of love.

You will come — you are coming — a thousand
 miles
Away, I can see you press through the aisles
 Of the forest, cool and gray ;
And my lips shall be dumb till our lips have met,
For never skill of a mortal yet,
To mortal words such music set,
 As beats in my heart to-day !

RETROSPECT.

O Loving One, O Bounteous One,
  What have I not received from Thee,
Throughout the seasons that have gone
  Into the past eternity!

For looking backward through the year,
  Along the way my feet have pressed,
I see sweet places everywhere,
  Sweet places, where my soul had rest.

And, though some human hopes of mine
  Are dead, and buried from my sight,
Yet from their graves immortal flowers
  Have sprung, and blossomed into light.

Body, and heart, and soul, have been
  Fed by the most convenient food ;
My nights are peaceful all the while,
  And all my mortal days are good.

My sorrows have not been so light,
  The chastening hand I could not trace ;
Nor have my blessings been so great
  That they have hid my Father's face.

HUMAN AND DIVINE.

VILE, and deformed by sin I stand,
    A creature earthy of the earth;
Yet fashioned by God's perfect hand,
    And in His likeness at my birth.

Here in a wretched land I roam,
    As one who had no home but this;
Yet am invited to become
    Partaker in a world of bliss.

A tenement of misery,
    Of clay is this to which I cling;
A royal palace waits for me,
    Built by the pleasure of my King!

My heavenly birthright I forsake, —
    An outcast, and unreconciled;
The manner of His love doth make
    My Father own me as His child.

Shortened by reason of man's wrong,
    My evil days I here bemoan;
Yet know my life must last as long
    As His, who struck it from his own.

Turned wholly am I from the way, —
    Lost, and eternally undone ;
I am of those, though gone astray,
    The Father seeketh through the Son.

I wander in a maze of fear,
    Hid in impenetrable night,
Afar from God, — and yet so near,
    He keeps me always in His sight.

I am as dross, and less than dross,
    Worthless as worthlessness can be ;
I am so precious that the cross
    Darkened the universe for me!

I am unfit, even from the dust,
    Master! to kiss thy garment's hem ;
I am so dear, that Thou, though just,
    Wilt not despise me nor condemn.

Accounted am I as the least
    Of creatures valueless and mean ;
Yet heaven's own joy shall be increased
    If e'er repentance wash me clean.

Naked, ashamed, I hide my face,
    All seamed by guilt's defacing scars ;
I may be clothed with righteousness
    Above the brightness of the stars.

Lord, I do fear that I shall go,
　Where death and darkness wait for me;
Lord, I believe, and therefore know
　I have eternal life in Thee!

THE PRIZE.

HOPE wafts my bark, and round my way
 Her pleasant sunshine lies;
For I sail with a royal argosy
 To win a royal prize.

A maiden sits in her loveliness
 On the shore of a distant stream,
And over the waters at her feet
 The lilies float, and dream.

She reaches down, and draws them in,
 With a hand that hath no stain;
And that lily of all the lilies, her hand,
 Is the prize I go to gain.

Her hair in a yellow flood falls down
 From her forehead low and white;
I would bathe in its billowy gold, and dream,
 In its sea of soft delight.

Her cheek is as fair as a tender flower,
 When its blushing leaves dispart;
Oh, my rose of the world, my regal rose,
 I must wear you on my heart!

I must kiss your lips, so sweetly closed
  O'er their pearly treasures fair;
Or strike on their coral reef, and sink
  In the waves of my dark despair!

TRIED AND TRUE.

OUR life is like a march, where some
 Fall early from the ranks, and die ;
And some, when times of conflict come,
 Go over to the enemy.

And he who halts upon the way —
 Wearied in spirit and in frame —
To call his roll of friends, will find
 How few make answer to their name !

And those who share our youth and joy,
 Not always keep our love and trust,
When days of awful anguish bow
 Our heads with sorrow to the dust.

My friend ! in such a fearful hour,
 When heart and spirit sank dismayed,
From thee the words of comfort came —
 From thee, the true and tender aid.

Therefore, though many another friend
 With youth and youthful pleasure goes,
Thou art of such as I would have
 Walk with me till life's solemn close.

Yea, with me when earth's trials are done, —
If I be found, when these shall cease,
Worthy to stand with those who wear
White raiment on the hills of peace.

THE HARMLESS LUXURY.

Her skies, of whom I sing, are hung
  With sad clouds, dropping saddest tears;
Yet some white days, like pearls, are strung
  Upon the dark thread of her years.

And as remembrance turns to slip
  Through fingers fond the treasures rare,
Ever her thankful heart and lip
  Run over into song and prayer.

With joys more exquisite and deep
  Than hers, she knows this good world teems,
Yet only asks that she may keep
  The harmless luxury of dreams.

Thankful that, though her life has lost
  The best it hoped, the best it willed,
Her sweetest dream has not been crossed,
  Or worse — but only half fulfilled.

And that beside her still, to wile
  Her thought from sad and sober truth,
Are Hope and Fancy, all the while
  Feeding her heart's éternal youth.

And who shall say that they who close
 Their eyes to Hope and Fancy's beams,
Are living truer lives than those,
 The dreamers, who believe their dreams!

A DAY DREAM.

If fancy do not all deceive,
   If dreams have any truth,
Thy love must summon back to me
   The glories of my youth;
For if but hope unto my thought
   Such transformation brings,
May not fruition have the power
   To change all outward things!

Come, then, and look into mine eyes
   Till faith hath left no doubt;
So shalt thou set in them a light
   That never can go out;
Or lay thy hand upon my hair,
   And keep it black as night;
The tresses that had felt that touch
   Would shame to turn to white.

To me it were no miracle,
   If, when I hear thee speak,
Lilies around my neck should bloom
   And roses in my cheek;

Or if the joy of thy caress,
  The wonder of thy smiles,
Smoothed all my forehead out again
  As perfect as a child's.

My lip is trembling with such bliss
  As mortal never heard ;
My heart, exulting to itself,
  Keeps singing like a bird ;
And while about my tasks I go
  Quietly all the day,
I could laugh out, as children laugh,
  Upon the hills at play.

O thou, whom fancy brings to me
  With morning's earliest beams,
Who walkést with me down the night,
  The paradise of dreams ;
I charge thee, by the power of love,
  To answer to love's call ;
Wake me to perfect happiness,
  Or wake me not at all !

OVER-PAYMENT.

I took a little good seed in my hand,
And cast it tearfully upon the land;
Saying, of this the fowls of heaven shall eat,
Or the sun scorch it with his burning heat.

Yet I, who sowed, oppressed by doubts and
      fears,
Rejoicing gathered in the ripened ears;
For when the harvest turned the fields to gold,
Mine yielded back to me a thousand-fold.

A little child begged humbly at my door;
Small was the gift I gave her, being poor,
But let my heart go with it; therefore we
Were both made richer by that charity.

My soul with grief was darkened, I was bowed
Beneath the shadow of an awful cloud;
When one, whose sky was wholly overspread,
Came to me asking to be comforted.

It roused me from my weak and selfish fears;
It dried my own to dry another's tears;
The bow, to which I pointed in his skies,
Set all my cloud with sweetest promises.

10

Once, seeing the inevitable way
My feet must tread, through difficult places
　　　lay;
I cannot go alone, I cried, dismayed, —
I faint, I fail, I perish, without aid!

Yet, when I looked to see if help were nigh,
A creature weaker, wretcheder than I,
One on whose head life's fiercest storms had
　　　beat,
Clung to my garments, falling at my feet.

I saw, I paused no more; my courage found,
I stooped and raised her gently from the
　　　ground;
Through every peril safe I passed at length,
For she who leaned upon me gave me strength.

Once, when I hid my wretched self from Him,
My Father's brightness seemed withdrawn and
　　　dim;
But when I lifted up mine eyes I learned
His face to those who seek is always turned.

A half-unwilling sacrifice I made;
Ten thousand blessings on my head were
　　　laid;
I asked a comforting spirit to descend;
God made himself my comforter and friend.

I sought His mercy in a faltering prayer,
And lo! His infinite tenderness and care,
Like a great sea, that hath no ebbing tide,
Encompassed me with love on every side!

PEACE.

O LAND, of every land the best —
    O Land, whose glory shall increase;
Now in your whitest raiment drest
    For the great festival of peace:

Take from your flag its fold of gloom,
    And let it float undimmed above,
Till over all our vales shall bloom
    The sacred colors that we love.

On mountain high, in valley low,
    Set Freedom's living fires to burn;
Until the midnight sky shall show
    A redder pathway than the morn.

Welcome, with shouts of joy and pride,
    Your veterans from the war-path's track;
You gave your boys, untrained, untried;
    You bring them men and heroes back!

And shed no tear, though think you must
    With sorrow of the martyred band;
Not even for him whose hallowed dust
    Has made our prairies holy land.

Though by the places where they fell,
  The places that are sacred ground,
Death, like a sullen sentinel,
  Paces his everlasting round.

Yet when they set their country free
  And gave her traitors fitting doom,
They left their last great enemy,
  Baffled, beside an empty tomb.

Not there, but risen, redeemed, they go
  Where all the paths are sweet with flowers;
They fought to give us peace, and lo!
  They gained a better peace than ours.

SUNSET.

Away in the dim and distant past
   That little valley lies,
Where the clouds that dimmed life's morning
      hours
   Were tinged with hope's sweet dyes.

That peaceful spot from which I looked
   To the future — unaware
That the heat and burden of the day
   Were meant for me to bear.

Alas, alas! I have borne the heat,
   To the burden learned to bow;
For I stand on the top of the hill of life.
   And I see the sunset now!

I stand on the top, but I look not back
   To the way behind me spread;
Not to the path my feet have trod,
   But the path they still must tread.

And straight and plain before my gaze
   The certain future lies;
But my sun grows larger all the while
   As he travels down the skies.

Yea, the sun of my hope grows large and
    grand;
For, with my childish years,
I have left the mist that dimmed my sight,
    I have left my doubts and fears.

And I have gained in hope and trust,
    Till the future looks so bright,
That, letting go of the hand of Faith,
    I walk, at times, by sight.

For we only feel that faith is life,
    And death is the fear of death,
When we suffer up to the solemn heights
    Of a true and living faith.

When we do not say, the dead shall rise
    At the resurrection's call;
But when we trust in the Lord, and know
    That we cannot die at all!

APOLOGY.

Nay, darling, darling, do not frown,
　　Nor call my words unkind ;
For my speech was but an idle jest,
　　As idle as the wind.

And now that I see your tender heart,
　　By my thoughtlessness is grieved,
I suffer both for the pain I gave,
　　And the pain that you received.

For if ever I have a thought of you,
　　That cold or cruel seems,
I have murdered my peace, and robbed my sleep
　　Of the joy of its happy dreams.

And when I have brought a cloud of grief
　　To your sweet face unaware,
Its shadow covers all my sky
　　With the blackness of despair.

And if in your pillow I have set
　　But one sharp thorn, alone,
That cruel, careless deed, transplants
　　A thousand to my own.

I grieve with your grief, I die in your frown,
  In your joy alone I live;
And the blow that it pained your heart to feel,
  It would break my own to give!

TWICE SMITTEN.

O DOUBLY-BOWED and bruisèd reed,
What can I offer in thy need?

O heart, twice broken with its grief,
What words of mine can bring relief?

O soul, o'erwhelmed with woe again,
How can I soothe thy bitter pain?

Abashed and still, I stand and see
Thy sorrow's awful majesty.

Only dumb silence may convey
That which my lip can never say.

I cannot comfort thee at all;
On the Great Comforter I call;

Praying that He may make thee see
How near He hath been drawn to thee.

For unto man the angel guest
Still comes through gates of suffering best;

And most our Heavenly Father cares
For whom He smites, not whom He spares.

So, to His chastening meekly bow,
Thou art of His beloved now!

A WOMAN'S ANSWER.

"Love thee?" Thou canst not ask of me
  So freely as I fain would give;
'T is woman's great necessity
  To love so long as she shall live;
Therefore, if thou dost lovely prove,
I cannot choose but give thee love!

"Honor thee?" By her reverence
  The truest woman best is known;
She needs must honor where she finds
  A nature loftier than her own;
I shall not turn from thee away,
Unless I find my idol clay!

"Obey?" Doth not the stronger will
  The weaker govern and restrain?
Most sweet obedience woman yields
  Where wisdom, power, manhood reign.
I'll give thee, if thou canst control,
The meek submission of my soul!

Henceforward all my life shall be
  Moulded and fashioned by thine own;

If wisdom, power, and constancy
   In all thy words and deeds are shown ;
Whether my vow be yea or nay,
I 'll " love, and honor, and obey."

THE SHADOW.

SHE was so good, we thought before she died
   To see new glory on her path descend;
And could not tell, till she had gone inside,
   Why there was darkness at her journey's end.

And then we saw that she had stood, of late,
   So near the entrance to that holy place,
That, from the Eternal City's open gate,
   The awful shadow fell across her face.

IN ABSENCE.

WATCH her kindly, stars:
From the sweet protecting skies
Follow her with tender eyes,
Look so lovingly that she
Cannot choose but think of me:
    Watch her kindly, stars!

    Soothe her sweetly, night:
On her eyes, o'erwearied, press
The tired lids with light caress;
Let that shadowy hand of thine
Ever in her dreams seem mine:
    Soothe her sweetly, night!

    Wake her gently, morn:
Let the notes of early birds
Seem like love's melodious words;
Every pleasant sound, my dear,
When she stirs from sleep should hear:
    Wake her gently, morn!

Kiss her softly, winds :
Softly, that she may not miss
Any sweet, accustomed bliss ;
On her lips, her eyes, her face,
Till I come to take your place,
Kiss and kiss her, winds !

MORNING AND AFTERNOON.

FAIR girl, the light of whose morning keeps
   The flush of its dawning glow,
Do you ask why that faded woman weeps
   Whose sun is sinking low?

You look to the future, on, above,
   She only looks to the past;
You are dreaming your first sweet dream of love,
   And she has dreamed her last.

You watch for feet that are yet to tread
   With yours, on a pleasant track;
She hears but the echoes dull and dread
   Of feet that come not back.

You are passing up the flowery slope,
   She left so long ago;
Your rainbows shine through the drops of hope,
   And hers through the drops of woe.

Your night in its visions glides away
   And at morn you live them o'er;
From her dreams by night and dreams by day
   She has waked to dream no more.

You are reaching forth with spirit glad
  To hopes that are still untried;
She is burying the hopes she had,
  That have slipped from her arms and died.

You think of the good, for you in store,
  Which the future yet wil! send;
While she, she knows it were well for her
  If she made a peaceful end!

ENCHANTMENT.

Her cup of life with joy is full,
  And her heart is thrilling so
That the beaker shakes in her trembling hand
  Till its sweet drops overflow.

All day she walks as in a trance;
  And the thought she does not speak,
But tries to hide from the world away,
  Burns out in her tell-tale cheek.

And often from her dreams of night
  She wakes to consciousness,
As the golden thread of her slumber breaks
  With the burden of its bliss.

She is almost troubled with the wealth
  Of a joy so great and good,
That she may not keep it to herself,
  Nor tell it if she would.

'T is strange that this should come to one
  Who, all her life before,
Content in her quiet household ways,
  Has asked for nothing more.

And stranger, that he, in whom the power,
　The wonderful magic lay,
That has changed her world to a paradise,
　Was a man but yesterday!

LIVING BY FAITH.

WHEN the way we should tread runs evenly on,
  And light as of noonday is over it all,
'T is strange how our feet will turn aside
  To paths where we needs must grope and
      fall;

How we suffer, knowing it all the while,
  Some phantom between ourselves and the
      light,
That shuts in disastrous, strange eclipse,
  The very powers of sense and sight.

Yet we live so, all of us, I think,
  Hiding whatever of truth we choose,
And deceiving ourselves with a subtilty
  That never a soul but our own could use.

We see the love in another's eyes,
  Where our own, reflected, is backward sent;
Or we hear a tone, that is not in a tone,
  And find a meaning that is not meant.

We put our faith in the help of those
  Who never have been a help at all;

And lean on an object that all the while
    We know we are holding back from its fall!

When words seem thoughtless, or deeds un-
    kind,
We are soothed with the kind intent instead;
And we say of the absent, silent one:
    He is faithful — but he is sick, or dead!

We have loved some dear familiar step,
    That once in its fall was firm and clear;
And that household music's sweetest sound
    Came fainter every day to our ear;

And then we have talked of the far-away —
    Of the springs to come and the years to be,
When the rose should bloom in our dear one's
    cheek,
    And her feet should tread in the meadows
    free!

We have turned from death, to speak of life,
    When we knew that earthly hope was past;
Yet thinking that somehow, God would work
    A miracle for us, to the last.

We have seen the bed of a cherished friend
    Pushed daily nearer and nearer, till
It stood at the very edge of the grave,
    And we looked across and beyond it, still.

Ay, more than this — we have come and gazed
 Down where that dear one's mortal part
Was lowered forever away from our sight;
 And we did not die of a broken heart.

Are we blind! nay, we know the world un-
   known
 Is all we would make the present seem;
That our Father keeps, till his own good time,
 The things we dream of, and more than we
   dream.

For we shall not sleep; but we shall be
   changed;
 And when that change at the last is made,
We shall bring realities face to face
 With our souls, and we shall not be afraid.

MY LADY.

As violets, modest, tender eyed,
The light of their beauty love to hide
    In deepest solitudes ;
Even thus, to dwell unseen, she chose,
My flower of womanhood, my rose,
    My lady of the woods !

Full of the deepest, truest thought,
Doing the very things she ought,
    Stooping to all good deeds :
Her eyes too pure to shrink from such,
And her hands too clean to fear the touch
    Of the sinfulest in his needs.

There is no line of beauty or grace
That was not found in her pleasant face,
    And no heart can ever stir,
With a sense of human wants and needs,
With promptings unto the holiest deeds,
    But had their birth in her.

With never a taint of the world's untruth
She lived from infancy to youth,
    From youth to womanhood ;

Taking no soil in the ways she trod,
But pure as she came from the hand of God,
 Before His face she stood.

My sweetest darling, my tenderest care!
The hardest thing that I have to bear
 Is to know my work is past;
That nothing now I can say or do
Will bring any comfort or aid to you, —
 I have said and done the last.

Yet I know I never was good enough,
That my tenderest efforts were all too rough
 To help a soul so fine;
So the lovingest angel among them all,
Whose touches fell, with the softest fall,
 Has pushed my hand from thine!

BORDER-LAND.

I KNOW you are always by my side
    And I know you love me, Winifred dear,
For I never called on you since you died,
    But you answered, tenderly, I am here!

So come from the misty shadows, where
    You came last night, and the night before,
Put back the veil of your golden hair,
    And let me look in your face once more.

Ah! it is you; with that brow of truth,
    Ever too pure for the least disguise ;
With the same dear smile on the loving mouth,
    And the same sweet light in the tender eyes.

You are my own, my darling still,
    So do not vanish or turn aside,
Wait till my eyes have had their fill, —
    Wait till my heart is pacified!

You have left the light of your higher place,
    And ever thoughtful, and kind, and good,
You come with your old familiar face,
    And not with the look of your angel-hood.

Still the touch of your hand is soft and light,
  And your voice is gentle, and kind, and low,
And the very roses you wear to-night,
  You wore in the summers long ago.

O world, you may tell me I dream or rave,
  So long as my darling comes to prove
That the feet of the spirit cross the grave,
  And the loving live, and the living love!

PASSING FEET.

ALL these hours she sits and counts,
　　As they pass her slow and sad,
Are the headsmen cutting off
　　Every flower of hope she had;

And the feet that come and go
　　In the darkness past her door,
If they trod upon her heart,
　　Could not pain it any more.

Friends hastening now to friends,
　　Faster as the night grows late;
Through all places men can go,
　　To all homes where women wait.

Some are pressing through the wood
　　Where the path is faint and new;
Some strike out a shorter way,
　　Across meadows wet with dew.

Some, along the highway's track,
　　Music to their foosteps keep;
Some are pushing into port,
　　From their exile on the deep.

But the hope she had at eve
   From her wretched soul has fled;
For the lamp of love she lit
   Has burned useless, and is dead.

So the feet that come and go,
   In the darkness past her door,
If they trod upon her heart
   Could not pain it any more!

OUR HOMESTEAD.

Our old brown homestead reared its walls
　From the wayside dust aloof,
Where the apple-boughs could almost cast
　Their fruit upon its roof;
And the cherry-tree so near it grew
　That when awake I 've lain
In the lonesome nights, I 've heard the limbs,
　As they creaked against the pane ;
And those orchard trees, oh those orchard trees !
　I 've seen my little brothers rocked
In their tops by the summer breeze.

The sweet-briar, under the window-sill,
　Which the early birds made glad,
And the damask rose, by the garden-fence,
　Were all the flowers we had.
I 've looked at many a flower since then,
　Exotics rich and rare,
That to other eyes were lovelier
　But not to me so fair ;
For those roses bright, oh those roses bright !
　I have twined them in my sister's locks,
That are hid in the dust from sight.

We had a well, a deep old well,
   Where the spring was never dry,
And the cool drops down from the mossy stones
   Were falling constantly ;
And there never was water half so sweet
   As the draught which filled my cup,
Drawn up to the curb by the rude old sweep
   That my father's hand set up.
And that deep old well, oh that deep old well !
   I remember now the plashing sound
Of the bucket as it fell.

Our homestead had an ample hearth,
   Where at night we loved to meet ;
There my mother's voice was always kind,
   And her smile was always sweet ;
And there I 've sat on my father's knee,
   And watched his thoughtful brow,
With my childish hand in his raven hair, —
   That hair is silver now !
But that broad hearth's light, oh that broad
      hearth's light !
   And my father's look, and my mother's smile,
They are in my heart to-night !

THE LADY JAQUELINE.

" FALSE and fickle, or fair and sweet,
   I care not for the rest,
The lover that knelt last night at my feet
   Was the bravest and the best.
Let them perish all, for their power has waned,
   And their glory waxèd dim ;
They were well enough while they lived and
     reigned,
   But never was one like him !
And never one from the past would I bring
   Again, and call him mine ; —
The King is dead, long live the King ! "
   Said the Lady Jaqueline.

" In the old, old days, when life was new,
   And the world upon me smiled,
A pretty, dainty, lover I had,
   Whom I loved with the heart of a child.
When the buried sun of yesterday
   Comes back from the shadows dim,
Then may his love return to me,
   And the love I had for him !
But since to-day hath a better thing
   To give, I 'll ne'er repine ; —

The King is dead, long live the King!"
Said the Lady Jaqueline.

" And yet it almost makes me weep,
  Ay ! weep, and cry, alas !
When I think of one who lies asleep
  Down under the quiet grass.
For he loved me well, and I loved again,
  And low in homage bent,
And prayed for his long and prosperous reign,
  In our realm of sweet content.
But not to the dead may the living cling,
  Nor kneel at an empty shrine ; —
The King is dead, long live the King!"
Said the Lady Jaqueline.

" Once, caught by the sheen of stars and lace,
  I bowed for a single day,
To a poor pretender, mean and base,
  Unfit for place or sway.
That must have been the work of a spell,
  For the foolish glamour fled,
As the sceptre from his weak hand fell
  And the crown from his feeble head ;
But homage true at last I bring
  To this rightful lord of mine, —
The King is dead, long live the King!"
Said the Lady Jaqueline.

12

" By the hand of one I held most dear,
　　And called my liege, my own !
I was set aside in a single year,
　　And a new queen shares his throne.
To him who is false, and him who is wed,
　　Shall I give my fealty ?
Nay, the dead one is not half so dead
　　As the false one is to me !
My faith to the faithful now I bring,
　　The faithless I resign ; —
The King is dead, long live the King ! "
　　Said the Lady Jaqueline.

Yea, all my lovers and kings that were
　　Are dead, and hid away,
In the past, as in a sepulchre,
　　Shut up till the judgment day.
False or fickle, or weak or wed,
　　They are all alike to me ;
And mine eyes no more can be misled, —
　　They have looked on royalty !
Then bring me wine, and garlands bring
　　For my king of the right divine ; —
The King is dead, long live the King ! "
　　Said the Lady Jaqueline.

LOVE'S RECOMPENSE.

HER heart was light as human heart can be,
  When blushingly she listened to the praise
  Of him who talked of love in those sweet days
When first she kept a lover's company.

That was hope's spring-time; now its flowers are
    dead,
  And she, grown tired of life before its close,
  Weaves melancholy stories out of woes,
Across whose dismal threads her heart has bled.

Yet even for such we need not quite despair,
  Since from our wrong God can bring forth
      His right;
  And He, though all are precious in His sight,
Doth give the uncared-for His peculiar care.

So, in the good life that shall follow this,
  He, being love, may make her love to be
  One golden thread, spun out eternally,
Through her white fingers, trembling with their
    bliss.

VAIN REPENTANCE.

Do we not say, forgive us, Lord,
　Oft when too well we understand
Our sorrow is not such as Thou
　Requirest at the sinner's hand?

Have we not sought Thy face in tears,
　When our desire hath rather been,
Deliverance from the punishment,
　Than full deliverance from the sin?

Alas! we mourn because we fain
　Would keep the things we should resign;
And pray, because we cannot pray, —
　Not my rebellious will, but Thine!

IN EXTREMITY.

Think on him, Lord! we ask Thy aid
   In life's most dread extremity;
For evil days have come to him,
   Who in his youth remembered Thee.

Look on him, Lord! for heart and flesh,
   Alike, must fail without Thy grace;
Part back the clouds, that he may see
   The brightness of his Father's face.

Speak to him, Lord! as Thou didst talk
   To Adam, in the Garden's shade,
And grant it unto him to hear
   Thy voice, and not to be afraid.

Support him, Lord! that he may come,
   Leaning on Thee, in faith sublime,
Up to that awful landmark, set,
   Between eternity and time.

And, Lord! if it must be that we
   Shall walk with him no more below,
Reach out of heaven Thy loving hand,
   And lead him where we cannot go.

THE LAST BED.

'T WAS a lonesome couch we came to spread
   For her, when her little life was o'er,
And a narrower one than any bed
   Whereon she had ever slept before.

And we feared that she could not slumber so,
   As we stood about her when all was done,
For the pillow seemed too hard and low
   For her precious head to rest upon.

But, when we had followed her two by two,
   And lowered her down there where she lies.
There was nothing left for us to do,
   But to hide it all from our tearful eyes.

So we softly and tenderly spread between
   Our face and the face our love regrets,
A covering, woven of leafy green,
   And spotted over with violets.

JEALOUSY.

I LOVE my love so well, I would
There were no eyes but mine that could
See my sweet piece of womanhood,
    And marvel of delight.

I dread that even the sun should rise;
That bold, bright rover of the skies,
Who dares to touch her closèd eyes,
    And put her dreams to flight.

No maid could be more kind to me,
No truer maiden lives than she,
But yet I die of jealousy,
    A thousand deaths in one.

I cannot bear to see her stop,
With her soft hand a flower to crop;
I envy even the clover-top
    Her dear foot treads upon.

How cruel in my sight to bless
Even her bird with the caress
Of fingers that I dare not press, —
    Those lady fingers, white;

That nestle oft in that dear place
Between her pillow and her face,
And, never asking leave or grace,
    Caress her cheek at night !

'T is torture more than I can bear
To see the wanton summer air
Lift the bright tresses of her hair,
    And careless let them fall.

The wind that through the roses slips,
And every sparkling dew-drop sips,
Without rebuke may kiss her lips,
    The sweetest rose of all.

I envy, on her neck of snow,
The white pearls hanging in a row,
The opals on her heart that glow,
    Flushed with a tender red.

I would not, in her chamber fair,
The curious stars should see her, where
I, even in thought, may scarcely dare
    For reverence to tread.

O maiden, hear and answer me
In kindness or in cruelty ;
Tell me to live, or let me die,
    I cry, and cry again !

Give me to touch one golden tress,
Give me thy white hand to caress,
Give me thy red, red lips to press,
   And ease my jealous pain!

SPRING AFTER THE WAR.

Come, loveliest season of the year,
   And every quickened pulse shall beat,
Your footsteps in the grass to hear,
   And feel your kisses, soft and sweet!

Come, and bestow new happiness
   Upon the heart that hopeful thrills;
Sing with the lips that sing for bliss,
   And laugh with children on the hills.

Lead dancing streams through meadows green.
   And in the deep, deserted dells
Where poets love to walk unseen,
   Plant flowers, with all delicious smells.

To humble cabins kindly go,
   And train your shady vines, to creep
About the porches, cool and low,
   Where mothers rock their babes to sleep.

But come with hushed and reverent tread,
   And bring your gifts, most pure and sweet,
To hallowed places where our dead
   Are sleeping underneath your feet.

There let the turf be lightly pressed,
   And be your tears that softly flow
The sweetest, and the sacredest,
   That ever pity shed for woe!

Scatter your holiest drop of dew,
   Sing hymns of sacred melody;
And keep your choicest flowers to strew
   The places where our heroes lie.

But most of all, go watch about
   The unknown beds of such as sleep,
Where love can never find them out,
   Nor faithful friendship come to weep.

Go where the ocean moans and cries,
   For those her waters hide from sight;
And where the billows heave and rise,
   Scatter the flowery foam-wreaths, white.

Ay, all your dearest treasures keep;
   We shall not miss them, but instead
Will give them joyfully, to heap
   The holy altars of our dead!

The poet from his wood-paths, wild,
   I know will take his sweetest flower,
The mother, singing to her child,
   Will strip the green vines from her bower;

The poor man from his garden bed
　The unpretending blooms will spare ;
The lover give the roses red
　He gathered for his darling's hair.

Yea, all thy gifts we love and prize
　We ask thee reverently to bring,
And lay them on the darkened eyes,
　That wait their everlasting spring !

THE WIFE'S CHRISTMAS.

How can you speak to me so, Charlie!
  It is n't kind, nor right;
You would n't have talked a year ago,
  As you have done to-night.

You are sorry to see me sit and cry,
  Like a baby vexed, you say;
When you did n't know I wanted a gift,
  Nor think about the day!

But I 'm not like a baby, Charlie,
  Crying for something fine;
Only a loving woman pained,
  Could shed such tears as mine.

For every Christmas time till now —
  And that is why I grieve —
It was you that wanted to give, Charlie,
  More than I to receive.

And all I ever had from you
  I have carefully laid aside;
From the first June rose you pulled for me,
  To the veil I wore as a bride.

And I would n't have cared to-night, Charlie,
  How poor the gift or small ;
If you only had brought me something to show
  That you thought of me at all.

The merest trifle of any kind,
  That I could keep or wear ;
A flimsy bit of lace for my neck,
  Or a ribbon for my hair.

Some pretty story of lovers true,
  Or a book of pleasant rhyme ;
A flower, or a holly branch, to mark
  The blessèd Christmas time.

But to be forgotten, Charlie !
  'T is that that brings the tear ;
And just to think, that I have n't been
  Your wife but a single year !

WOOED AND WON.

THE maiden has listened to loving words.
　　She has seen a heart like a flower unclose;
And yet she would almost hide its truth,
　　And shut the leaves of the blushing rose.

For the spell of enchantment is broken now,
　　And all the future is seen so clear,
That she longs for the very longing gone,
　　For the restless pleasure of hope and fear.

She stands so close to her painting now
　　That its smallest failings are revealed, —
Ah, that beautiful picture, that looked so sweet,
　　By the misty distance half concealed!

" Alas," she says, " can it then be true
　　That all is vanity, as they preach, —
That the good is in striving after the good,
　　And the best is the thing we never reach?

" Are not the sweetest words we can speak:
　　' It is mine, and I hold my treasure fast?'
And the saddest wrung from the human heart:
　　' It might have been, but the time is past?'

"I do not know, and I will not say,
    But yet of a truth it seems to me,
I would give my certain knowledge back,
    For my hope, with its sweet uncertainty!"

SONG.

I SEE him part the careless throng,
  I catch his eager eye;
He hurries towards me where I wait, —
  Beat high, my heart, beat high!

I feel the glow upon my cheek,
  And all my pulses thrill;
He sees me, passes careless by; —
  Be still, my heart, be still!

He takes another hand than mine,
  It trembles for his sake;
I see his joy, I feel my doom; —
  Break, O my heart-strings, break!

MY RICHES.

THERE is no comfort in the world
  But I, in thought, have known ;
No bliss for any human heart,
  I have not dreamed my own ;
And fancied joys may sometimes be
More real than reality.

I have a house in which to live,
  Pleasant, and fair, and good,
Its hearth is crowned with warmth and light.
  Its board with daintiest food.
And I, when tired with care or doubt,
Go in and shut my sorrows out.

I have a father, one whose care
  Goes with me where I roam ;
A mother, waiting anxiously
  To see her child come home ;
And sisters, from whose tender eyes
The love in mine hath sweet replies.

I have a friend, who sees in me
  What none beside can see,

Not faultless, but as firm and true,
   And pure, as man may be;
A friend, whose love is never dim,
And I can never change to him.

My boys are very gentle boys,
   And after they are grown,
They're nobler, better, braver men
   Than any I have known!
And all my girls are fair and good
From infancy to womanhood.

So with few blessings in the world
   That men can see or name,
Home, love, and all that love can bring
   My mind has power to claim;
And life can never cease to be
A good and pleasant thing to me.

THE BOOK OF NATURE.

We scarce could doubt our Father's power,
  Though his greatness were untold
In the sacred record made for us
  By the prophet-bards of old.

We must have felt his watchfulness
  About us everywhere;
Though we had not learned, in the Holy Word,
  How he keeps us in his care.

I almost think we should know his love,
  And dream of his pardoning grace,
If we never had read how the Saviour came,
  To die for a sinful race.

For the sweetest parables of truth
  In our daily pathway lie,
And we read, without interpreter,
  The writing on the sky.

The ravens, fed when they clamor, teach
  The human heart to trust;
And the rain of goodness speaks, as it falls
  On the unjust and the just.

The sunshine drops, like a leaf of gold,
   From the book of light above;
And the lily's missal is written full
   Of the words of a Father's love.

So, when we turn from the sacred page
   Where the holy record lies,
And its gracious plans and promises
   Are hidden from our eyes;

One open volume still is ours,
   To read and understand;
And its living characters are writ
   By our Father's loving hand!

I CANNOT TELL.

Once, being charmèd by thy smile,
 And listening to thy praises, such
As women, hearing all the while,
 I think could never hear too much, —

I had a pleasing fantasy
 Of souls that meet, and meeting blend,
And hearing that same dream from thee.
 I said I loved thee, O my friend!

That was the flood-tide of my youth,
 And now its calm waves backward flow;
I cannot tell if it were truth,
 If what I feel be love or no.

My days and nights pass pleasantly,
 Serenely on my seasons glide,
And though I think and dream of thee,
 I dream of many things beside.

Most eagerly thy praise is sought,
 'T is sweet to meet, and sad to part;
But all my best and deepest thought
 Is hidden from thee in my heart.

And still the while a charm or spell,
  Half holds, and will not let me go;
'T is strange, and yet I cannot tell
  If what I feel be love, or no!

DEAD LOVE.

WE are face to face, and between us here
   Is the love we thought could never die;
Why has it only lived a year?
   Who has murdered it — you or I?

No matter who — the deed was done
   By one or both, and there it lies;
The smile from the lip forever gone,
   And darkness over the beautiful eyes.

Our love is dead, and our hope is wrecked;
   So what does it profit to talk and rave,
Whether it perished by my neglect,
   Or whether your cruelty dug its grave!

Why should you say that I am to blame,
   Or why should I charge the sin on you?
Our work is before us all the same,
   And the guilt of it lies between us two.

We have praised our love for its beauty and
     grace;
   Now we stand here, and hardly dare

To turn the face-cloth back from the face,
   And see the thing that is hidden there.

Yet look! ah, that heart has beat its last,
   And the beautiful life of our life is o'er,
And when we have buried and left the past,
   We two, together, can walk no more.

You might stretch yourself on the dead, and
      weep,
   And pray as the Prophet prayed, in pain ;
But not like him could you break the sleep,
   And bring the soul to the clay again.

Its head in my bosom I can lay,
   And shower my woe there, kiss on kiss,
But there never was resurrection-day
   In the world for a love so dead as this!

And, since we cannot lessen the sin
   By mourning over the deed we did,
Let us draw the winding-sheet up to the chin,
   Ay, up till the death-blind eyes are hid!

FIGS OF THISTLES.

As laborers set in a vineyard
　Are we set in life's field,
To plant and to garner the harvest
　Our future shall yield.

And never since harvests were ripened,
　Or laborers born,
Have men gathered figs of the thistle,
　Or grapes of the thorn!

Even he who has faithfully scattered
　Clean seed in the ground,
Has seen, where the green blade was growing,
　Tares of evil abound.

Our labor ends not with the planting,
　Sure watch must we keep,
For the enemy sows in the night-time
　While husbandmen sleep.

And sins, all unsought and unbidden,
　Take root in the mind;
As the weeds grow, to choke up the blossoms,
　Chance-sown by the wind.

But no good crop, our hands never planted,
  Doth Providence send ;
Nor doth that which we planted have increase
  Till we water and tend.

By our fruits, whether good, whether evil,
  At last are we shown ;
And he who has nothing to gather,
  By his lack shall be known.

And no useless creature escapeth
  His righteous reward ;
For the tree or the soul that is barren
  Is cursed of the Lord !

COMING ROUND.

'T is all right, as I knew it would be by and by ;
We have kissed and made up again, Archie
        and I ;
And that quarrel, or nonsense, whatever you will,
I think makes us love more devotedly still.

The trouble was all upon my side, you know ;
I 'm exacting sometimes, rather foolishly so ;
And let any one tell me the veriest lie
About Archie, I 'm sure to get angry and cry.

Things will go on between us again just 'the
        same, —
For as *he* explains matters he was n't to blame ;
But 't is useless to tell you ; I can't make you see
How it was, quite as plainly as he has made me.

You thought "I would make him come round
        when we met ! "
You thought " there were slights I could never
        forget ! "
Oh you did ! let me tell you, my dear, to
        your face,
That your thinking these things does n't alter
        the case !

You "can tell what I said?" I don't wish you
    to tell!
You know what a temper I have, very well;
That I'm sometimes unjust to my friends who
    are best;
But *you've* turned against Archie the same as
    the rest!

"Why hasn't he written? what kept him so
    still?" —
His silence was sorely against his own will;
He has faults, that I own; but he, he wouldn't
    deceive;
He was ill, or was busy, — was both, I believe!

Did he flirt with that *lady?* I s'pose I should
    say,
Why, yes, — when she threw herself right in
    the way;
He was led off, was foolish, but that is the
    worst, —
And she was to blame for it all, from the first.

And he's *so* glad to come back again, and to
    find
A woman once more with a heart and a mind;
For though others may please and amuse for
    an hour,
I hold all his future — his life — in my power!

And now, if things don't go persistently wrong,
Our destinies cannot be parted for long ;
For he said he would give me his fortune and
　　　name, —
Not those words, but he told me what meant
　　　just the same.

So what could I do, after all, at the last,
But just ask him to pardon my doubts in the
　　　past ;
For though *he* had been wrong, I should still,
　　　all the same,
Rather take it myself than let him bear the
　　　blame.

And, poor fellow ! he felt so bad, I could not
　　　bear
To drive him by cruelty quite to despair ;
And so, to confess the whole truth, when I
　　　found
He was willing to do so himself, *I* came round !

PECCAVI.

I HAVE sinned, I have sinned, before thee, the
    Most Holy!
And I come as a penitent, bowing down lowly,
With my lips making freely their awful admis-
    sion,
And mine eyes raining bitterest tears of con-
    trition;
And I cry unto thee, with my mouth in the
    dust:
        O God! be not just!

O God! be not just; but be merciful rather, —
Let me see not the face of my Judge but my
    Father:
A sinner, a culprit, I stand self-convicted,
Yet the pardoning power is thine unrestricted;
I am weak; thou art strong; in thy goodness
    and might,
        Let my sentence be light!

I have turned from all gifts which thy kindness
    supplied me,
Because of the one which thy wisdom denied
    me;

I have bandaged mine eyes — yea, mine own
    hands have bound me ;
I have made me a darkness, when light was
    around me ;
And I cry by the wayside : O Lord ! that I
    might
        Receive back my sight !

For the sake of my guilt, may my guilt be
    forgiven,
And because mine iniquities mount unto heaven !
Let my sins, which are crimson, be snow in
    their brightness ;
Let my sins, which are scarlet, be wool in their
    whiteness.
I am out of the way, and my soul is dismayed —
        I am lost, and afraid.

I have sinned, and against Him whose justice
    may doom me ;
Insulted His power whose wrath can consume
    me ;
Yet, by that blest name by which angels adore
    Him —
That name through which mortals may dare
    come before Him —
I come, saying only, My Father above,
        My God, be thou Love !

OTWAY.

Poet, whose lays our memory still
  Back from the past is bringing,
Whose sweetest songs were in thy life
  And never in thy singing;

For chords thy hand had scarcely touched
  By death were rudely broken,
And poems, trembling on thy lip,
  Alas! were never spoken.

We say thy words of hope and cheer
  When hope of ours would languish,
And keep them always in our hearts
  For comfort in our anguish.

Yet not for thee we mourn as those
  Who feel by God forsaken;
We would rejoice that thou wert lent,
  Nor weep that thou wert taken.

For thou didst lead us up from earth
  To walk in fields elysian,
And show to us the heavenly shore
  In many a raptured vision.

14 .

Thy faith was strong from earth's last trial
The spirit to deliver,
And throw a golden bridge across
Death's dark and silent river;

A bridge, where fearless thou didst pass
The stern and awful warder,
And enter with triumphant songs
Upon the heavenly border.

Oh for a harp like thine to sing
The songs that are immortal;
Oh for a faith like thine to cross
The everlasting portal!

Then might we tell to all the world
Redemption's wondrous story;
Go down to death as thou didst go,
And up from death to glory.

IMPATIENCE.

WILL the mocking daylight never be done?
   Is the moon her hour forgetting?
O weary sun! O merciless sun!
   You have grown so slow in setting!

And yet, if the days could come and go
   As fast as I count them over,
They would seem to me like years, I know,
   Till they brought me back my lover.

Down through the valleys, down to the south,
   O west wind, go with fleetness,
Kiss, with your daintiest kisses, his mouth,
   And bring to me all its sweetness.

Go when he lieth in slumber deep,
   And put your arms about him,
And hear if he whisper my name in his sleep,
   And tell him, I die without him.

O birds, that sail in the air like ships,
   To me such discord bringing,
If you heard the sound of my lover's lips,
   You would be ashamed of your singing!

O rose, from whose heart such a crimson rain
  Up to your soft cheek gushes,
You never could show your face again,
  If you saw my lover's blushes!

O hateful stars, in hateful skies,
  Can you think your light is tender,
When you steal it all from my lover's eyes,
  And shine with a borrowed splendor?

O sun, going over the western wall,
  If you stay there none will heed you;
For why should you rise or shine at all
  When he is not here to need you?

Will the mocking daylight never be done?
  Is the moon her hour forgetting?
O weary sun! O merciless sun!
  You have grown so slow in setting!

THE LAMP ON THE PRAIRIE.

THE grass lies flat beneath the wind
   That is loosed in its angry might,
Where a man is wandering, faint and blind,
   On the prairie, lost at night.

No soft, sweet light of moon or star,
   No sound but the tempest's tramp;
When suddenly he sees afar
   The flame of a friendly lamp!

And hope revives his failing strength,
   He struggles on, succeeds, —
He nears a humble roof at length,
   And loud for its shelter pleads.

And a voice replies, " Whoever you be
   That knock so loud at my door,
Come in, come in! and bide with me
   Till this dreadful storm is o'er.

" And no wilder, fiercer time in March
   Have I seen since I was born;

If a wolf for shelter sought my porch
    To-night, he might lie till morn."

As he enters, there meets the stranger's gaze
    One bowed by many a year, —
A woman, alone by the hearth's bright blaze,
    Tending her lamp anear.

" Right glad will I come," he said, "for the
        sweep
    Of the wind is keen and strong ;
But tell me, good neighbor, why you keep
    Your fire ablaze so long ?

" You dwell so far from the beaten way
    It might burn for many a night ;
And only belated men, astray,
    Would ever see the light."

" Ay, ay, 't is true as you have said,
    But few this way have crossed ;
But why should not fires be lit and fed
    For the sake of men who are lost ?

" There are women enough to smile when they
        come,
    Enough to watch and pray
For those who never were lost from home,
    And never were out of the way.

" And hard it were if there were not some
    To love and welcome back
The poor misguided souls who have gone
    Aside from the beaten track.

" And if a clear and steady light
    In my home had always shone,
My own good boy had sat to-night
    By the hearth, where I sit alone.

" But alas! there was no faintest spark
    The night when he should have come ;
And what had he, when the pane was dark,
    To guide his footsteps home ?

" But since, each night that comes and goes,
    My beacon fires I burn ;
For no one knows but he lives, nor knows
    The time when he may return ! "

" And a lonesome life you must have had,
    Good neighbor, but tell me, pray,
How old when he went was your little lad ?
    And how long has he been away ? "

" 'T is thirty years, by my reckoning,
    Since he sat here last with me ;
And he was but twenty in the spring, —
    He was only a boy, you see !

" And though never yet has my fire been low,
  Nor my lamp in the window dim,
It seems not long to be waiting so,
  Nor much to do for him !

" And if mine eyes may see the lad
  But in death, 't is enough of joy ;
What mother on earth would not be glad
  To wait for such a boy !

" You think 't is long to watch at home,
  Talking with fear and doubt ;
But long is the time that a son may roam
  Ere he tire his mother out !

" And if you had seen my good boy go,
  As I saw him go from home,
With a promise to come at night, you would
    know
  That, some good night, he would come."

" But suppose he perished where never pass
  E'en the feet of the hunter bold,
His bones might bleach in the prairie grass
  Unseen till the world is old ! "

" Ay, he might have died : you answer well
  And truely, friend, he might ;
And this good old earth on which we dwell
  Might come to an end to-night !

" But I know that here in its place, instead,
    It will firm and fast remain ;
And I know that my son, alive or dead,
    Will return to me again !

" So your idle fancies have no power
    To move me or appall ;
He is likelier now to come in an hour
    Than never to come at all !

" And he shall find me watching yet,
    Return whenever he may ;
My house has been in order set
    For his coming many a day.

" You were rightly shamed if his young feet
        crossed
    That threshold stone to-night,
For your foolish words, that he might be lost,
    And his bones be hid from sight !

" And oh, if I heard his light step fall,
    If I saw him at night or morn
Far off, I should know my son from all
    The sons that ever were born.

" And, hark ! there is something strange about,
    For my dull old blood is stirred ;
That was n't the feet of the storm without,
    Nor the voice of the storm I heard !

"It was but the wind! nay, friend, be still,
  Do you think that the night wind's breath
Through my very soul could send a thrill
  Like the blast of the angel, Death?

"'T is my boy! he is coming home, he is near,
  Or I could not hear him pass;
For his step is as light as the step of the deer
  On the velvet prairie grass.

"How the tempest roars! how my cabin rocks!
  Yet I hear him through the din;
Lo! he stands without the door — he knocks —
  I must rise and let him in!"

She rose — she stood erect, serene;
  She swiftly crossed the floor;
And the hand of the wind, or a hand unseen,
  Threw open wide the door.

Through the portal rushed the cruel blast,
  With a wail on its awful swell;
As she cried, "My boy, you have come at last!"
  And prone o'er the threshold fell.

And the stranger heard no other sound,
  And saw no form appear;
But whoever came at the midnight found
  Her lamp was burning clear!

COMPENSATION.

CROOKED and dwarfed the tree must stay,
Nor lift its green head to the day,
Till useless growths are lopped away,

And thus doth human nature do;
Till it hath careful pruning, too,
It cannot grow up straight and true.

For, but for chastenings severe,
No soul could ever tell how near
God comes, to whom He loveth, here.

Without life's ills, we could not feel
The blessèd change from woe to weal;
Only the wounded limb can heal.

The sick and suffering learn below,
That which the whole can never know,
Of the soft hand that soothes their woe.

And never man is blest as he,
Who, freed from some infirmity,
Rejoices in his liberty.

He sees, with new and glad surprise,
The world that round about him lies,
Who slips the bondage from his eyes;

And comes from where he long hath lain,
Comes from the darkness and the pain,
Out into God's full light again.

They only know who wait in fear
The music of a footstep near,
Falling upon the listening ear.

And life's great depths are soonest stirred
In him who hath but seldom heard
The magic of a loving word.

Joy after grief is more complete;
And kisses never fall so sweet
As when long-parted lovers meet.

One who is little used to such,
Surely can tell us best how much
There is in a kind smile or touch.

'T is like the spring wind from the south,
Or water to the fevered mouth,
Or sweet rain falling after drouth.

By him the deepest rest is won
Who toils beneath the noonday sun
Faithful until his work is done.

And watchers through the weary night
Have learned how pleasantly the light
Of morning breaks upon the sight.

Perchance the jewel seems most fair
To him whose patient toil and care
Has brought it to the upper air.

And other lips can never taste
A draught like that he finds at last
Who seeks it in the burning waste.

When to the mother's arms is lent,
That sweet reward for suffering sent
To her, from the Omnipotent,

I think its helpless, pleading cry
Touches her heart more tenderly,
Because of her past agony.

We learn at last how good and brave
Was the dear friend we could not save,
When he has slipped into the grave.

And after He has come to hide
Our lambs upon the other side,
We know our Shepherd and our Guide.

And thus, by ways not understood,
Out of each dark vicissitude,
God brings us compensating good.

For Faith is perfected by fears,
And souls renew their youth with years,
And Love looks into heaven through tears.

OUR GOOD PRESIDENT.

Our sun hath gone down at the noonday,
    The heavens are black;
And over the morning, the shadows
    Of night-time are back.

Stop the proud boasting mouth of the cannon;
    Hush the mirth and the shout; —
God is God! and the ways of Jehovah
    Are past finding out.

Lo! the beautiful feet on the mountains,
    That yesterday stood,
The white feet that came with glad tidings
    Are dabbled in blood.

The Nation that firmly was settling
    The crown on her head,
Sits like Rizpah, in sackcloth and ashes,
    And watches her dead.

Who is dead? who, unmoved by our wailing,
    Is lying so low?
Oh my Land, stricken dumb in your anguish,
    Do you feel, do you know,

That the hand which reached out of the darkness
 Hath taken the whole;
Yea, the arm and the head of the people, —
 The heart and the soul?

And that heart, o'er whose dread awful silence
 A nation has wept;
Was the truest, and gentlest, and sweetest,
 A man ever kept.

Why, he heard from the dungeons, the rice-fields,
 The dark holds of ships
Every faint, feeble cry which oppression
 Smothered down on men's lips.

In her furnace, the centuries had welded
 Their fetter and chain;
And like withes, in the hands of his purpose,
 He snapped them in twain.

Who can be what he was to the people, —
 What he was to the state?
Shall the ages bring to us another
 As good and as great?

Our hearts with their anguish are broken,
 Our wet eyes are dim;
For us is the loss and the sorrow,
 The triumph for him!

For, ere this, face to face with his Father
  Our martyr hath stood;
Giving into His hand a white record,
  With its great seal of blood!

15

CHRISTMAS.

O TIME by holy prophets long foretold,
Time waited for by saints in days of old,
    O sweet, auspicious morn
    When Christ, the Lord, was born !

Again the fixèd changes of the year
Have brought that season to the world most
        dear,
    When angels, all aflame,
    Bringing good tidings came.

Again we think of her, the meek, the mild,
The dove-eyed mother of the holy child,
    The chosen, and the best,
    Among all women blest.

We think about the shepherds, who, dismayed,
Fell on their faces, trembling and afraid,
    Until they heard the cry,
    Glory to God on high !

And we remember those who from afar
Followed the changing glory of the star
    To where its light was shed
    Upon the sacred head ;

And how each trembling, awe-struck worshiper,
Brought gifts of gold, and frankincense, and
  myrrh,
  And spread them on the ground
  In reverence profound.

We think what joy it would have been to share
In their high privilege who came to bear
  Sweet spice and costly gem
  To Christ, in Bethlehem.

And in that thought we half forget that He
Is wheresoe'er we seek him earnestly;
  Still filling every place
  With sweet, abounding grace.

And though in garments of the flesh, as then,
No more he walks this sinful earth with men,
  The poor, to him most dear,
  Are always with us here.

And He saith, Inasmuch as ye shall take
Good to these little ones for my dear sake,
  In that same measure ye
  Have brought it unto Me!

Therefore, O men in prosperous homes who live,
Having all blessings earthly wealth can give,
  Remember their sad doom
  For whom there is no room —

No room in any home, in any bed,
No soft white pillow waiting for the head,
    And spare from treasures great
    To help their low estate.

Mothers whose sons fill all your homes with
    light,
Think of the sons who once made homes as
    bright,
    Now laid in sleep profound
    On some sad battle-ground ;

And into darkened dwellings come with cheer,
With pitying hand to wipe the falling tear,
    Comfort for Christ's dear sake
    To childless mothers take !

Children whose lives are blest with love untold,
Whose gifts are greater than your arms can hold,
    Think of the child who stands
    To-day with empty hands !

Go fill them up, and you will also fill
Their empty hearts, that lie so cold and still,
    And brighten longing eyes
    With grateful, glad surprise.

May all who have, at this blest season seek
His precious little ones, the poor and weak,

In joyful, sweet accord,
Thus lending to the Lord.

Yea, Crucified Redeemer, who didst give
Thy toil, thy tears, thy life, that we might live,
Thy Spirit grant, that we
May live one day for Thee!

SUGAR-MAKING.

THE crocus rose from her snowy bed
　　As she felt the Spring's caresses,
And the willow from her graceful head
　　Shook out her yellow tresses.

Through the crumbling walls of his icy cell
　　Stole the brook, a happy rover;
And he made a noise like a silver bell
　　In running under and over.

The earth was pushing the old dead grass
　　With lily hand from her bosom,
And the sweet brown buds of the sassafras
　　Could scarcely hide the blossom

And breaking Nature's solitude
　　Came the axe strokes clearly ringing,
For the chopper was busy in the wood
　　Ere the early birds were singing.

All day the hardy settler now
　　At his tasks was toiling steady;
His fields were cleared, and his shining plow
　　Was set by the furrow ready.

And down in the woods, where the sun appeared
  Through the naked branches breaking,
His rustic cabin had been reared
  For the time of sugar-making.

And now, as about it he came and went,
  Cheerfully planning and toiling,
His good·child sat there, with eyes intent
  On the fire and the kettles boiling.

With the beauty Nature gave as her dower,
  And the artless grace she taught her,
The woods could boast no fairer flower,
  Than Rose, the settler's daughter.

She watched the pleasant fire anear,
  And her father coming and going,
And her thoughts were all as sweet and clear
  As the drops his pail o'erflowing.

For she scarce had dreamed of earthly ills,
  And love had never found her;
She lived shut in by the pleasant hills
  That stood as a guard around her;

And she might have lived the self-same way
  Through all the springs to follow,
But for a youth, who came one day
  Across her in the hollow.

He did not look like a wicked man,
   And yet, when he saw that blossom,
He said, "I will steal this Rosé if I can,
   And hide it in my bosom."

That he could be tired you had not guessed
   Had you seen him lightly walking;
But he must have been, for he stopped to rest
   So long that they fell to talking.

Alas! he was athirst, he said,
   Yet he feared there was no slaking
The deep and quenchless thirst he had
   For a draught beyond his taking.

Then she filled the cup and gave to him,
   The settler's blushing daughter,
And he looked at her across the brim
   As he slowly drank the water.

And he sighed as he put the cup away,
   For lips and soul were drinking;
But what he drew from her eyes that day
   Was the sweetest, to his thinking.

I do not know if her love awoke
   Before his words awoke it;
If she guessed at his before he spoke,
   Or not until he spoke it.

But howsoe'er she made it known,
  And howsoe'er he told her,
Each unto each the heart had shown
  When the year was little older.

For oft he came her voice to hear,
  And to taste of the sugar-water;
And she was a settler's wife next year
  Who had been a settler's daughter.

And now their days are fair and fleet
  As the days of sugar weather,
While they drink the water, clear and sweet,
  Of the cup of life together.

MY FRIEND.

O my friend, O my dearly belovèd!
    Do you feel, do you know,
How the times and the seasons are going;
    Are they weary and slow?
Does it seem to you long, in the heavens,
    My true, tender mate,
Since here we were living together,
    Where dying I wait.
'T is three years, as we count by the spring-times,
    By the birth of the flowers,
What are years, aye! eternities even,
    To love such as ours?
Side by side are we still, though a shadow
    Between us doth fall;
We are parted, and yet are not parted,
    Not wholly, and all.
For still you are round and about me,
    Almost in my reach,
Though I miss the old pleasant communion
    Of smile and of speech.
And I long to hear what you are seeing,
    And what you have done,
Since the earth faded out from your vision,
    And the heavens begun;

Since you dropped off the darkening fillet
  Of clay from your sight,
And opened your eyes upon glory
  Ineffably bright!
Though little my life has accomplished,
  My poor hands have wrought;
I have lived what has seemed to be ages
  In feeling and thought,
Since the time when our path grew so narrow,
  So near the unknown,
That I turned back from following after,
  And you went on alone.
For we speak of you cheerfully, always,
  As journeying on;
Not as one who is dead do we name you;
  We say, you are gone.
For how could we speak of you sadly,
  We, who watched while the grace
Of eternity's wonderful beauty
  Grew over your face!

Do we call the star lost that is hidden
  In the great light of morn?
Or fashion a shroud for the young child
  In the day it is born?
Yet behold this were wise to their folly,
  Who mourn, sore distressed,
When a soul, that is summoned, believing,
  Enters into its rest!

And for you, never any more sweetly
    Went to rest, true and deep,
Since the first of our Lord's blessèd martyrs
    Having prayed, fell asleep.

What to you was the change, the transition,
    When looking before,
You felt that the places which knew you
    Should know you no more?
Did the soul rise exultant, ecstatic?
    Did it cry, all is well?
What it was to the left and the loving
    We only can tell.
'T was as if one took from us sweet roses
    And we caught their last breath;
'T was like any thing beautiful passing, —
    It was not like death!
Like the flight of a bird, when still rising,
    And singing aloud,
He goes towards the summer-time, over
    The top of the cloud.
Now seen and now lost in the distance,
    Borne up and along,
From the sight of the eyes that are watching
    On a trail of sweet song.
As sometimes, in the midst of the blackness,
    A great shining spark
Flames up from the wick of a candle,
    Blown out in the dark;

So while we were watching and waiting,
　'Twixt hoping and doubt,
The light of the soul flashed upon us,
　When we thought it gone out.
And we scarce could believe it forever
　Withdrawn from our sight,
When the cold lifeless ashes before us
　Fell silent and white!
Ah! the strength of your love was so wondrous
　So great was its sway,
It forced back the spirit half-parted
　Away from the clay;
In its dread of the great separation,
　For not then did we know,
Love can never be left, O belovèd,
　And never can go!

As when from some beautiful casement
　Illumined at night,
While we steadfastly gaze on its brightness,
　A hand takes the light;
And our eyes still transfixed by the splendor
　Look earnestly on,
At the place where we lately beheld it,
　Even when it has gone:
So we looked in your soul's darkening windows,
　Those luminous eyes,
Till the light taken from them fell on us
　From out of the skies!

Though you wore something earthly about you
　　That once we called you,
A robe all transparent, and brightened
　　By the soul shining through :
Yet when you had dropped it in going,
　　'T was but yours for a day,
Safe back in the bosom of Nature
　　We laid it away.
Strewing over it odorous blossoms
　　Their perfume to shed,
But you never were buried beneath them,
　　And never were dead !
What we brought there and left for the darkness
　　Forever to hide,
Was but precious because you had worn it,
　　And put it aside.
As a garment might be, you had fashioned
　　In exquisite taste ;
A book which your touch had made sacred,
　　A flower you had graced.
For all that was yours we hold precious,
　　We keep for your sake
Every relic our saint on her journey
　　Has not needed to take.

Who that knew what your spirit, though fettered,
　　Aspired to, adored,
When as far as the body would loose it
　　It mounted and soared ;

What soul in the world that had loved you,
    Or known you aright,
Would look for you down in the darkness,
    Not up in the light?
Why, the seed in the ground that we planted,
    And left there to die,
Being quickened, breaks out of its prison,
    And grows towards the sky.
The small fire that but slowly was kindled,
    And feebly begun,
Gaining strength as it burns, flashes upward,
    And mounts to the sun.
And could such a soul, free for ascending,
    Could that luminous spark,
Blown to flame by the breath of Jehovah,
    Go out in the dark?
Doth the bird stay behind when the window
    Wide open is set?
Or, freed from the snare of the fowler,
    Hasten back to his net?
And you pined in the flesh, being burdened
    By its great weight of ills,
As a slave, who has tasted wild freedom,
    Still pines for the hills.
And therefore it is that I seek you
    In full, open day,
Where the universe stretches the farthest
    From darkness away.
And think of you always as rising
    And spurning the gloom;

All the width of infinity keeping
    'Twixt yourself and the tomb!

Sometimes in white raiment I see you,
    Treading higher and higher,
On the great sea of glass, ever shining,
    And mingled with fire.
With the crown and the harp of the victor,
    Exultant you stand;
And the melody drops, as if jewels
    Dropped off from your hand.
You walk in that beautiful city,
    Adorned as a bride,
Whose twelve gates of pearl are forever
    Opened freely and wide.
Whose walls upon jasper foundations
    Shall firmly endure;
Set with topaz, and beryl, and sapphire,
    And amethyst pure.
You are where there is not any dying,
    Any pain, any cries;
And God's hand has wiped softly foreve,
    The tears from your eyes:
For if spirits because of much loving
    Come nearest the throne,
You must be with the saints and the children
    Our Lord calls his own!

Sometimes you are led in green pastures,
    The sweetest and best;

Sometimes as a lamb in the bosom
  Of Jesus you rest.
Where you linger the spiciest odors
  Of paradise blow,
And under your feet drifts of blossoms
  Lie soft as the snow.
If you follow the life-giving river,
  Or rest on its bank,
You are set round by troops of white lilies,
  In rank after rank.
And the loveliest things, and the fairest,
  That near you are seen
Seem as beautiful handmaids, who wait on
  The step of a queen.
For always, wherever I see you,
  Below or above,
I think all the good which surrounds you
  Is born of your love.
And the best place is that where I find you,
  The best thing what you do;
For you seem to have fashioned the heaven.
  That was fashioned for you!

But as from His essence and nature
  Our God, ever blest,
Cannot do any thing for His children
  But that which is best;
And till He hath gathered them to Him,
  In the heavens above,

16

Cannot joy over them as one singing,
　　Nor rest in His love;
So you, who have drawn from His goodness
　　Your portion of good,
Must help where your hand can be helpful,
　　Cannot rest if you would;
For you could not be happy in heaven,
　　By glory shut in,
While any soul whom you might comfort
　　Should suffer and sin.
So unto the heirs of salvation
　　Have you freely appeared;
And the earth by your sweet ministration
　　Is brightened and cheered.

I am sure you are near to the dying!
　　For often we mark
A smile on their faces, whose brightness
　　Lights the soul through the dark;
Sure, that you have for man in his direst
　　Necessity cared;
Preparing him then for whatever
　　The Lord hath prepared.
So, whenever you tenderly loosen
　　A hand from our grasp,
We feel, you can hold it and keep it
　　More safe in your clasp;
And that he, whose dear smile for a season,
　　Our love must resign,

Gains the infinite comfort and sweetness
  Of love such as thine.

Yea, lost mortal, immortal forever!
  And saved evermore!
You revisit the world and the people,
  That saw you of yore.
To the sorrowful house, to the death-room,
  The prison and tomb,
You come, as on wings of the morning,
  To scatter the gloom.
Wherever in desolate places
  Earth's misery abides;
Wherever in dark habitations
  Her cruelty hides;
If there the good seek for the wretched,
  And lessen their woes,
Surely they are led on by the angels,
  And you are of those.

In the holds of oppression, where captives
  Sit silent and weep,
Your face as the face of a seraph
  Has shined on their sleep:
And your white hand away from the dungeon
  His free step has led,
When the slave slipped his feet from the fetters,
  And the man rose instead;
Free, at least in his dreams and his visions,

That one to behold,
Who walked through the billows of fire
  With the faithful of old.
And what are the walls of the prison,
  The rack and the rod,
To him, who in thought and in spirit,
  Bows only to God?
If his doors are swung back by the angels,
  That visit his sleep —
If his singing ascend at the midnight,
  Triumphant and deep;
He is freer than they who have bound him,
  For his spirit may rise
And as far as infinity reaches
  May travel the skies!

And who knows but the wide world of slumber
  Is real as it seems?
God giveth them sleep, His belovèd,
  And in sleep giveth dreams!
And happy are we if such visions
  Our souls can receive;
If we sleep at the gateway of heaven,
  And wake and believe.
If angels for us on that ladder
  Ascend and descend,
Whose top reaches into the heavens,
  With God at the end!
If our souls can raise up for a Bethel

E'en the great stone that lies
    At the mouth of the sepulchre, hiding
      Our dead from our eyes!
But alas! if our sight be withholden,
      If faithless, bereft,
We stoop down, looking in at the grave-clothes
      The Risen hath left;
And see not the face of the angel
      All dazzling and white,
Who points us away from the darkness,
      And up to the light!
And alas! when our Helper is passing,
      ,If then we delay,
To cast off the hindering garments
      And follow his way!

Yet how blindly humanity gropeth,
      While clad in this veil;
When we seek for the truths that are nearest,
      How often we fail.
How little we learn of each other,
      How little we teach;
How poorly the wisest interpret
      The look and the speech!
Only that which in nearest communion
      We give and receive,
That which spirit to spirit imparteth,
      Can we know and believe.

Thus I know that you live, live forever,
　Free from death, free from harms;
For in dreams of the night, and at noonday
　Have you been in my arms!
And I know that, when I shall be like you,
　We shall meet face to face;
That all souls, who are joined by affection,
　Are joined by God's grace;
And that, oh my dearly belovèd,
　But the Father above,
Who made us and joined us can part us;
　And He cannot for love!

RECONCILED.

O YEARS, gone down into the past;
  What pleasant memories come to me,
Of your untroubled days of peace,
  And hours almost of ecstasy!

Yet would I have no moon stand still,
  Where life's most pleasant valleys lie;
Nor wheel the planet of the day
  Back on his pathway through the sky.

For though, when youthful pleasures died,
  My youth itself went with them, too;
To-day, ay! even this very hour,
  Is the best time I ever knew.

Not that my Father gives to me
  More blessings than in days gone by;
Dropping in my uplifted hands
  All things for which I blindly cry:

But that his plans and purposes
  Have grown to me less strange and dim;
And where I cannot understand,
  I trust the issues unto Him.

And, spite of many broken dreams,
   This have I truly learned to say, —
The prayers I thought unanswered once,
   Were answered in God's own best way.

And though some dearly cherished hopes
   Perished untimely ere their birth,
Yet have I been beloved and blessed
   Beyond the measure of my worth.

And sometimes in my hours of grief,
   For moments I have come to stand
Where in the sorrows on me- laid,
   I felt a loving Father's hand.

And I have learned, the weakest ones
   Are kept securest from life's harms;
And that the tender lambs alone
   Are carried in the shepherd's arms.

And, sitting by the way-side blind,
   He is the nearest to the light,
Who crieth out most earnestly,
   "Lord, that I might receive my sight!"

O feet, grown weary as ye walk,
   Where down life's hill my pathway lies,
What care I, while my soul can mount,
   As the young eagle mounts the skies!

O eyes, with weeping faded out,
   What matters it how dim ye be?
My inner vision sweeps untired
   The reaches of eternity!

O death, most dreaded power of all,
   When the last moment comes, and thou
Darkenest the windows of my soul,
   Through which I look on Nature now;

Yea, when mortality dissolves,
   Shall I not meet thine hour unawed?
My house eternal in the heavens
   Is lighted by the smile of God!

www.ingramcontent.com/pod-product-compliance
Lightning Source LLC
Chambersburg PA
CBHW030758020726

47499CB00006B/1679